Neither Here
Nor There

Miriam Drori

CROOKED
CAT

Discover us online:
www.crookedcatpublishing.com

Join us on facebook:
www.facebook.com/crookedcatpublishing

Tweet a photo of yourself holding
this book to **@crookedcatbooks**
and something nice will happen.

For David,
who let me follow my dreams.

The Author

Miriam Drori was born and raised in London, but for most of her life she has lived in Jerusalem, where she married and gave birth to three now-grown-up children. She studied Maths at Royal Holloway, University of London, and worked as a computer programmer and later as a technical writer, a profession that blends technical skills with writing.

Unlike most writers, Miriam didn't always yearn to write fiction. As a late developer who was always the youngest in the class, she was made to feel she had no aptitude for writing while at school. Now she is making up for that. She has been studying the art of writing for several years, online, in writing groups and in workshops, and has had some short stories published. Neither Here Nor There is her first novel.

Miriam began writing in order to raise awareness of social anxiety and never fails to mention this common but little-known disorder when the opportunity arises.

Acknowledgements

Several people made this novel possible and I will always be grateful to them.

Gill Downs, who has been my friend, advisor and supporter ever since we remet twelve years ago.

David Brauner and Judy Labensohn, who taught me about writing.

Sally Quilford, who ran the excellent pocket novel workshop that led me to consider writing a romance.

Sue Barnard and Gail Richards, who spared no time or effort in helping to turn my draft into a real novel.

David Drori, who pointed out several problems when I thought there were no more left.

Laurence and Steph Patterson of Crooked Cat Publishing, who accepted me into their warm basket of cats and used their professional expertise to produce a volume of high calibre.

Thank you to all, and to everyone else who gave me encouragement along the way.

Miriam Drori
May 2014

Neither Here
Nor There

This novel is a work of fiction that makes no statement about any groups of people. In particular, the author does not imply any generalisation or stereotyping of the haredi community.

Chapter One

Esty's insides turned somersaults as she crossed the familiar street, stepping on the lines of the light railway. In one sense, nothing had changed. Walking along Jaffa Road to the main post office was something she'd done many times. Her clothes – skirt well below the knees, sleeves that covered her elbows, black tights – were the ones she was used to, her handbag the one she usually carried.

And yet, in her mind, Esty knew that today couldn't be more different. The first day of a completely different life. Her handbag might look the same as usual to any observer, but she knew it contained documents she would need on the other side. In her purse was all the money she'd managed to put together without making anyone suspicious. She was about to be a different person – the person she'd long felt she should have been.

But she wasn't there yet. Now, she was in limbo, neither here nor there.

At the entrance to the post office, Esty opened her bag for the security guard and felt a sudden shock wave pass through her. Would he wonder why she was carrying all those documents? A moment later she reproached herself. Idiot. He's not looking for documents.

Esty passed through the metal detector and retrieved her bag. So far so good. Now what? To the right was a shop selling stationery, mobile phones and stamp albums. She remembered as a child being fascinated by the exotic stamps, knowing she could look but never buy. To the left was a large room with counters along one wall and rows of seats, many of them occupied. She didn't want to ask questions, to have people

3

remember her if 'they' came looking for her. Would they do that? She wasn't sure. Best to avoid people who worked here if possible.

She walked across the large hall, doing her best to keep her eyes averted from all the people. At the other end of the room she passed through an open doorway and saw what she wanted – a row of telephones in a deserted corridor. But… how did you use these phones? The pictures seemed to show inserting a card. What sort of card? A credit card? Whatever it was, Esty didn't have one. How could she find out what to do?

Back in the main hall, people were sitting clutching tickets and waiting for their number to be called. Esty had seen this before – at the healthcare clinic, for instance. Did she have to take a ticket from the machine and wait, just to ask her silly question? She glanced at the people sitting there. Some of them were like her – or rather, like she had been. What if one of them recognised her and started talking to her? That would be awful. And how was she going to manage now? How was she going to solve the phone problem? She blinked a tear away.

The young man – where had he come from? He'd asked her something. What was it? Was she all right?

"Yes. That is…" She wouldn't have pursued it, but there was something about his face. It showed kindness, and worry… worry about her, even though he wasn't one of her people… her former people. "Do you know how those phones work… how you pay for the call?"

She gestured to the corridor, and he went back there with her and examined one of the phones. "I think you need a phone card. You can probably buy it at one of the counters." Despite all her anxieties, Esty noticed the foreign accent in his Hebrew speech. He sounded like a native English speaker, but not American – possibly English. She recognised the almost-not-existent R sound, as opposed to the American nasal one, and the Israeli one rolled at the back of the throat. And she noticed his voice – so pleasant-sounding and gentle. Such concern in those deep brown eyes.

Esty glanced towards the counters. She must have still looked worried, because the man said, "Would you like to use my mobile? It's all right," he added, holding it out to her when he saw Esty hesitating.

"Thank you." Esty felt her cheeks burning as she took the phone.

With his arm, the man pointed to the rows of seats. "I'll wait for you in there."

So nice of him to let her make the call in private, but… Esty frowned at the contraption in her hand. "How do you…?"

"Press the numbers and then press this button. Is it here in Jerusalem?"

Esty nodded.

"So press zero-two and then the number."

As the man left her for the other room, Esty took the pencil and paper out of her pocket and unfolded the paper to see the number, although she really knew it by heart. How silly of her. The person she needed to call probably was in Jerusalem, but the number was a mobile. She'd never owned a mobile phone herself, but she'd made phone calls to people with mobile phones before and knew that mobile numbers began with zero-five. She could feel her heart racing, but nevertheless managed to follow the nice man's instructions and suddenly there was a ringing tone and the voice of another man. "Hello?"

Heart pounding, she recited the piece she'd rehearsed many times. "My name is Esty Sherman and I've just left my home in the ultra-orthodox… the haredi community and I don't want to go back there. I want to be secular. Can you help me? Is this the right place?"

"Yes, this is the right place, but I have to ask you some questions first. How old are you?"

"Nineteen." Despite her thumping heart, Esty noticed the man's gentle, friendly tones.

"Are you married?"

"No."

"Who knows that you're doing this?"

"No one."

"I see. I have to explain, Esty. We are a voluntary organisation that helps people who leave the haredi community, but we don't persuade or encourage anyone to leave. That's a decision you have to make by yourself. You could go back now and no one would know you ever thought of leaving. If you continue, you run a very big risk of cutting yourself off from your friends and family – even your parents."

"I understand that."

"If you do leave, things will be very hard for you at first. In the worst-case scenario, you'll want to change your mind and go back, but they won't accept you any more. Are you prepared for that?"

"Yes. I've thought about it and I'm sure I want to do this."

"Esty, if you have any doubts, then go back now while you still can."

"No, I want to go ahead with it. I know it'll be hard, but I'm absolutely certain it's the right thing for me to do."

"In that case, I'm going to give you my address. I want you to go there now and I'll meet you there. My name is Avi – Avi Slonim. Do you have a pen and paper?"

"Yes."

Avi gave Esty an address in the neighbourhood of Malcha. Esty had heard of Malcha from occasional visits to the Jerusalem Mall – the large shopping centre to the south west of the city. She remembered looking up at the newish blocks of flats all over the hillside and wondering what it would be like to live in them, with those families. It would be a completely different sort of life, she'd been sure of that. She remembered musing how babies begin life so similar but very quickly become a part of their environment. If she'd been born to one of those families, for instance, she'd have worn different clothes, attended different schools, learnt different subjects, kept different traditions and held different beliefs. Only a quirk of fate – or God's will, as she'd always thought of it – had determined the family she would be born into. Now she was about to visit one of those flats, where she'd see for herself how those families lived.

"Where are you now?" Avi asked.

"At the main post office."

"You have to take the number seventeen bus. The easiest way for you is to walk or ride along Jaffa Road to Davidka Square and catch the bus from there. Take the seventeen going towards the Malcha Mall and get off four stops after the shopping centre. Of course, the bus might not stop at all of them, so you'd be better off asking for my street. Can you manage that?"

"Yes." Normally, that would be easy for Esty. She'd taken buses, even outside the city. She'd often visited her father's parents in Bnei Brak, the religious town close to secular Tel-Aviv. On the bus there had often been secular people, too. Sometimes she'd sat next to a secular woman, but she'd never spoken to one. In the summertime, she'd observed the bare legs beneath a short skirt and the bare arms, wondering if the clothes were worn for comfort or to lure men as her teachers sometimes implied.

But this day was far from normal, and the short bus journey she had to undertake made her anxious. Above all, she was terrified of meeting someone she knew. How would she handle it?

"Good. I'll see you there then."

Esty removed the phone from her ear and was just wondering how to end the call when the young man reappeared. He must have been watching her, but Esty was sure he couldn't have heard anything.

"I didn't know how to…"

"That's okay." He took the phone back, pressed a button and slipped it into his pocket.

"Thank you so much."

"No problem. Will you be all right now?" The man tilted his head a little and raised his eyebrows, causing Esty to feel a flutter inside over the continuing somersaults.

"Oh yes. Thank you." Esty managed a smile before rushing off to begin her journey.

Stepping out of the post office, Esty began to retrace her steps back along Jaffa Road, walking round the dawdlers and shop window gazers and the people waiting for the next train.

The man in the post office had lightened her mood. He was proof that there were good people on the other side of the divide she was crossing. More than ever, she felt ready for her new future, whatever it held in store for her. And she would face it with her head held high.

As she looked up from the pavement, her smile vanished. Coming towards her was her worst nightmare, in the form of Mrs Greenspan.

Chapter Two

Mark Langer watched the girl until she disappeared past the far doorway. Why? Why had he felt so strange, so incomprehensibly weird in her presence? Why did he have such a strong sense of disappointment now that she'd gone, never to be seen again? Surely he couldn't have any amorous feelings for one such as her. And yet....

Suddenly Mark realised he probably looked silly standing there, motionless, staring at an image that was no longer there – as if the film had stuck just before she'd turned and left his line of vision. He made his way to the back row of seats and sat down.

What was it that had made him approach this girl in the first place? It wasn't like him at all. He always preferred not to interfere, expecting that no one needed or wanted any assistance he might have been able to give, afraid he'd merely be in the way. Only last week Claude, one of his flatmates, had teased him for his reticence.

"Mark, why you go to your room? Why you no stay to talk?"

"You were with a girl. I didn't like to intrude."

"Oh you British." Claude had wrung his hands in mock despair. "You are so... so... *réservé*."

Mark hadn't mentioned to Claude how many times people had told him how British he was, and how that was getting on his nerves. The people he'd met in Britain differed from one another as much as people could anywhere. He never felt it was possible to generalise about them in any way. Yet here, in Israel, they were all thought of as a sort of cartoon replica of P.G. Wodehouse's Bertie Wooster, or was it Jeeves, the butler? Local imitations of this caricature of the British consisted of raising the normal pitch and saying, "Would you like a cup of tea?" in an attempt at an accent Mark had heard only in clips of the Queen from the 1950s. Like Claude, Israelis seemed to think the British were all reserved, and unfortunately, Mark's natural diffidence did nothing to dispel that belief.

But today, somehow, was different. Mark had seen the girl standing there, looking as if she'd burst out crying at any moment, and without thinking he'd gone over to her and offered to help. Far from rejecting it, she'd seemed pleased at the offer and he'd felt so happy and proud of himself for having thought of letting her use his mobile phone.

What was it about the girl that drew him to her, he wondered, conjuring up her image in his mind. Her small, slim stature? Her blue, expressive eyes? Her long, camel-coloured hair tied back in a ponytail? Yes, all of those. But most of all, it was her smile, because it made her pretty face perfect. It was so genuine, and showed her obvious delight at his small act of kindness.

Mark hadn't been in this country, in this city, for a year yet, but he was beginning to get used to certain things. Like the way you could bump into the most unlikely people. Only the other day, a young man had stepped away from a group of tourists to greet him. Mark had been embarrassed to admit he hadn't recognised him, but the man didn't seem to mind. He reminded Mark they'd been at school together. He sounded happy and excited, explaining how much he was enjoying his tour of the Holy Land with other members of his church.

Maybe in the same way, Mark thought, he might bump into this girl again. That would be wonderful....

Then reality hit him, as if he'd felt a bang on the head by one of those plastic hammers he'd seen in the hands of children during the Israeli Independence Day celebrations the previous month. Crazy! He almost said the word out loud. What was he thinking of? He'd seen the way the girl was dressed – long skirt, long sleeves, black tights on a hot summer's day at the very end of May. He knew that meant she had to be orthodox. He'd never had much connection with orthodox Jews, either back in England or here in Jerusalem, but he knew enough to understand that there could never be anything between him and that girl.

Mark glanced at his watch. Almost 6.30. He'd planned to go home and grab a bite to eat before going out to his folk dancing group. He took his ticket out of his trouser pocket and compared the number on it with the one on the indicator board. He'd missed his turn at the counter. Never mind. He could buy the stamps tomorrow. He stood up and strode purposefully out of the post office.

***

Try as he might, Mark couldn't get the girl out of his mind. He wandered home in a daze. He even found himself in a collision with a pram. "Watch where you're going," called the mother, rather crossly, over the sound of a crying baby. Mark mumbled an apology and escaped the scene as quickly as he could, his cheeks burning and not from the sun.

Back at home, Claude had to remove a smoking frying pan from a gas ring turned up high. "Hey, you wanna make fire? You want that we die?"

Then Claude looked straight into Mark's eyes. "What happen to you?"

"Nothing," said Mark, dreamily.

"Pah! I know what those eyes mean. You cannot hide it from Claude. *C'est l'amour. Oui?*"

Mark collapsed onto the kitchen stool and looked up at Claude. "You're right. There was a girl. A girl who is pretty and sweet and has the most delightful smile. But there could never be anything between that girl and me. And besides, I'll never see her again."

"You know, in French we have an expression. Never say

11

never."

Mark nodded to show comprehension rather than agreement. "We have the same expression in English."

***

Mark sat down on a bench when the couple dancing began. Couple dancing was a problem. He hadn't learnt the couple dances as well as he'd learnt the circle dances because he didn't always find a partner – sometimes he did, other times he didn't. When he did, he usually found pleasure in interacting with one other person, whoever she was. Between the dances, there was often time to talk – nothing deep, of course, only a few pleasantries, but all the same, it was enjoyable.

This evening he didn't have the mental energy to try to find a partner. He didn't want to face the rejections – "No, I'm dancing with…" or simply "No." It was the latter type that he feared most. It made him think: Why? What's wrong with me?

And once again he found himself thinking of that girl in the post office. He imagined her as his dancing partner, saw them learning the steps together. If only….

He didn't notice the woman coming towards him, and didn't hear her speak over the loud music. She tapped him on the shoulder and asked again, "Do you want to dance with me?"

Mark hesitated for a moment. He'd got to know many of the regular dancers, at least by sight. Some of them seemed to know every dance. Those ones usually also performed very well and were a pleasure to watch. But he never danced with them; they were way out of his league. Then at the other end of the scale were those who, despite attending regularly, never managed to remember the steps of any dance. Mark sometimes wondered why such people wanted to keep coming. Surely they realised that they weren't suited to this hobby.

This woman was one of those. Mark had danced with her in the past and hadn't particularly enjoyed it. This evening he felt he didn't have the patience for her. He replied in the only way he could think of. "No." Then, because that sounded much too harsh, he added, "Sorry."

Chapter Three

In the tight-knit community in which Esty had been brought up, everyone knew everyone. And the women often bumped into each other – at the synagogue, in the street, in food and clothes shops. When they met, they gossiped. They asked after each other, after their families, with friendly concern. Esty's mother, Rivka, joined in the chats as much as the others, now thoroughly at home with this culture she'd adopted.

But Rivka was always wary of Mrs Greenspan and others like her. "Be careful what you say to Mrs Greenspan," she'd say to Esty. "That woman might sound as if she's merely passing the time of day, but she's nosy. Very, very nosy. She wants to know all the details, just in case there's some intrigue going on, some juicy piece of news that she can spread around the community. So be cordial with her but not too friendly. Not that we have anything to hide," Rivka added, "but that woman could twist a flat plain into a mountain."

Now, with every step, the tall, thin woman was coming nearer and this time Esty did have something to hide. If this secret got out, it would ruin everything. How was she going to manage? She fixed a smile on her face and prepared to meet the busybody.

Mrs Greenspan lost no time. "Esty, how lovely to see you. How are you? And how's your dear mother? I remember she was feeling poorly." Her whiny voice and exaggerated intonation showed her apparent sympathy for what it was – false.

Esty hoped her inner turmoil was invisible. "Thank God, she's much better now."

"I'm so glad. Ooh, it almost slipped my mind. Congratulations on your younger sister's engagement. She must be so happy."

"Thank you. Yes, she is." The smile was still fixed on Esty's face.

"And what about you? Is there no young man in sight?"

Esty felt her cheeks starting to burn. "Not yet."

"Oh dear. You could try a different matchmaker. I can recommend one."

"Thank you, Mrs Greenspan, but I don't think that will be necessary."

"Oh. Well I'm sure, with God's help, you will find a good and pious husband. The trick is not to be too picky. Remember, time doesn't stand still and the longer you wait the less choice you will have. You wouldn't want to get past the age of eighteen and still have no husband in sight, would you? How old are you now?"

"Nineteen."

"Oh dear, that's bad." The woman tutted her fake compassion. "Very bad."

Esty couldn't think of a response to this. She desperately wanted to escape the virtual clutches of this frightening woman.

"Shouldn't you be at home now, helping your poor mother?"

Esty forced herself to concentrate. Oh yes. Thursday afternoon. Time to prepare for the Sabbath. And her mother hadn't been well. "I… I had to go to the post office on my way back from work." Esty hoped she wouldn't ask why. She didn't want to lie.

"Why…."

Esty cut her off. "Excuse me, Mrs Greenspan, but I'm in rather a hurry."

"Of course. I wish your mother a complete recovery."

Esty hurried off but remained on full alert. She'd managed to get away from Mrs Greenspan, but there might well be others, just as dangerous. As she waited at the traffic light to cross over to Davidka Square, she kept her eyes down and prayed to God to keep her safe. Then she remembered that God was no longer there to protect her and suddenly felt very vulnerable. Life was going to be very scary, but if other people managed without God then so could she.

Reaching the other side, Esty found the correct bus stop and stood a little way off, worried that someone she knew might see her and wonder where she was going. When the bus arrived, she merged with the throng of people climbing on, pleased that there were still some journeys remaining on her electronic card. Moving to the back of the bus, she sank into an empty seat and squeezed herself against the window. She kept her head down and fixed her eyes on the bag she clutched on her lap. 'They' could be anywhere. The woman who'd sat down next to her could be an informant....

When her heart began to beat a little more slowly, Esty put her hand in her pocket and took out the piece of paper on which she'd written Avi's address. She would have to ask the bus driver where to get off once they'd passed the indoor shopping centre. But what a street name. Rehov Hanachash – Snake Street. Did the name signify something? Was she being lured into a trap to receive a fatal bite?

Enough superstition, Esty told herself. Next you'll be adding up the values of the letters in Hanachash to determine your future. Esty sighed. *Gematria*. It was something the rabbis often did. Because Hebrew letters were also used for the Hebrew numbering system, they'd add up the values of the letters in a word or phrase and use the meaning of another word or phrase whose letters added up to the same value to prove a point.

When Esty was little, she believed everything they said. But later she began to suspect that the rabbis manipulated the words or phrases until the results worked out for them. She even calculated her own examples of gematria that produced completely different results – in some cases even questioning the very existence of God. She never discussed these with anyone. She told herself it was wrong to even think of these things and endeavoured to rid herself of such thoughts and be a better person.

Until now. Esty would never have any use for gematria again, neither the good sort nor the bad. Still, it was hard to forget the habits of a lifetime, even if that lifetime was only nineteen years long.

***

The bus driver stopped for Esty and pointed across the street when she asked for Rehov Hanachash. He seemed to eye her rather curiously, as if he thought she didn't belong in this place, but he didn't say anything else.

Following the bus driver's direction, she soon found the flat she was looking for, with the name Slonim on a wooden sign fixed to the door. At least something turned out to be easy on this difficult day. On the way, she'd noticed a few people and some had noticed her, frowning at her. Suddenly she felt out of place. It wasn't that she hadn't seen people dressed in this way before, but those people had always been amongst those who dressed in a familiar way – like her parents and teachers and everyone she knew. Now, it was she who was the weird one. She felt them staring at her, although she may have imagined it. That bus driver was right; she didn't belong here. Not the way she looked just now. This must be what it feels like to be alone in a strange land, she thought. Yes, she was alone in a strange land at the end of a single, short bus ride.

A man answered her ring. "Are you Esty?"

When she nodded, he opened the door wider. "Come in."

Esty noticed the *mezuzah* fixed to the doorway, but stopped herself from putting her hand to it and then kissing the fingers that had touched it. That belonged to her previous life, that act of kissing the piece of parchment enclosed in a case that identified Jewish homes. But she hesitated when the man said, "I'm Avi," and held out his hand for her to shake.

Immediately, the hand returned to Avi's side. "Don't worry, I understand. It takes time to get used to new ways."

They were joined by a woman whom Avi introduced as his wife, Liat. "Pleased to meet you," said Liat, holding out her hand.

Esty shook it and relaxed a bit. She always felt more comfortable with women, because she didn't have to be afraid of accidentally touching them, or doing or saying anything that would be deemed inappropriate. Could she really get used to a lifestyle in which men and women touched each other freely?

Despite feeling more comfortable with Liat, Esty noted the glaring differences between her and her mother. Liat was wearing trousers and a sleeveless top. Esty's mother always wore a skirt that covered her knees and sleeves that covered her elbows. And her hair was always covered, usually with a wig, another symbol of the modesty women were supposed to display. Liat's shoulder-length black hair hung loose. Esty could tell it wasn't a wig because it was too close to the head and it was greying. Besides, there was no reason why she would wear a wig with those clothes and in that place, and of course Esty didn't expect her to. It was just that everything felt so strange.

"Come into the living room," said Avi, "and I'll tell you what's going to happen."

They sat on armchairs and Avi explained. "In a few minutes, we'll have a light, milk meal. Liat is preparing it now. Will you have some? I'm afraid we don't keep kosher."

Again Esty hesitated. She'd never eaten anything in a house that wasn't not just kosher but glatt kosher – allowing only food approved by the strictest authorities. She knew that eating in a non-kosher house was allowed, but only under the most stringent conditions. It had to be food that she herself had examined and found to be acceptable, and it had to be served on disposable plates and eaten with disposable cutlery.

But that was the old life – the life she'd just broken away from. "Yes, thank you," she heard herself say, albeit quietly. At least if he said it was a milk meal, there wouldn't be any meat, she assumed. These people might not always have separated milk and meat for themselves, she argued to herself, but presumably they would know enough about keeping kosher to understand that "milk meal" wouldn't include meat.

"In the meantime," Avi continued, "I'm going to try to find a family you can stay with. I'm really sorry that we can't have you to stay here, but we have three teenage children who take up all the space."

To Esty, this place seemed large enough for a lot more than three children.

"If I don't find anyone this evening, you can sleep on our sofa tonight and we'll find you a family tomorrow." Avi reached for the telephone.

The first two families Avi tried weren't able to take Esty. "It's a difficult time, right before the summer holidays," Avi explained.

Esty bit her lip. "I'm sorry I have to be such a burden."

"Not at all," said Avi. "These are all families who have volunteered to help people just like you. We'll find a family in the end and they'll be pleased to have the opportunity to set you on your feet. Don't worry."

The next family Avi called agreed to take Esty. As it happened, they lived nearby.

***

It was hard to push the food down and Esty wasn't sure why. The cheese pie was tasty enough. It could be her ordeal today that put her off food, or thoughts of her unknown future. It could be the fight she was having with herself to eat it despite all the prohibitions that had been drummed into her.

"Won't you have some more?" Liat asked, indicating the dish.

"No, thank you. It's lovely, but I'm in such a state, it's hard to eat."

Liat nodded sympathetically. "Try some ice cream. That should go down easily."

The ice cream did slip down, and while Esty ate it, Avi explained her options. "Our organisation arranges meetings, so you'll get to know others who've been in your situation. It also provides limited subsidies for education. But I'm afraid the subsidies are only available after you've been out of your community for at least a year. In the meantime, you'll have to find work to support yourself. Do you have any idea what you could do?"

"I've worked in a kindergarten. I love looking after little children."

"That's a possibility. We could look into that. Do you have any qualifications?"

"I didn't take the matriculation exams, if that's what you mean. We didn't learn any maths or Hebrew literature or other secular subjects. But I do know English."

"Really? How's that?"

"My mother comes from England. I always spoke English with her and she taught me to read and write, too. I don't know why it was important to her. I've never used it outside the house."

"Well, it's going to be very useful for you now, with English being one of the compulsory subjects in the matriculation. If you want to take it, that is."

"Do you think I should?"

"You won't get far without it. But studying costs money. I assume you don't have the funds for that?"

Esty shook her head.

"So you'll have to wait for at least a year. Unless…. Do you have any relatives who aren't haredi?"

Esty nodded. "My grandparents in London. My mother broke away from them when she came to Israel for a visit and decided to stay. That's when she became orthodox."

"And now you're doing the opposite."

The simple sentence caught Esty by surprise. She hadn't thought about it like that before. She'd only thought about breaking away from the only way of life she'd known up to now. Really, she was completing the cycle begun by her mother. "Yes, I suppose I am. But I don't know if my grandparents even want to know me. I've never spoken to them."

"You won't know unless you contact them. Do you have an address or phone number for them?"

Occasional letters had arrived from England. Esty had never read them, but she'd seen the name and an address in a place called Hampstead on the backs of the envelopes, and had memorised the details. She nodded. "I'll write to them."

Liat, who'd gone out of the room with the dishes, returned with a large plastic bag. "I found some clothes we don't need. I think they should fit you."

Esty, who hadn't even thought as far as the fact that she'd need clothes, found herself breaking into a smile. "Thank you. That's so kind."

"Not at all." Liat shook her head, making light of her good deed.

***

Standing outside the front door of her new, temporary home, her handbag hanging from one shoulder, the plastic bag of second-hand clothes dangling from the other hand, Esty felt like a refugee. In fact, she mused, that's exactly what she was, having just escaped from a place she could never return to. The strange thing was, she'd hardly gone any distance. She was still in the town she'd been born in – the one she'd always lived in. So near and yet so far.

Her journey to this place had been much shorter and easier to plan and carry out than those undertaken by people who fled their countries and suffered hardship while attempting to reach their ultimate destination. Much, much shorter than the forty years the Children of Israel spent wandering in the desert before they reached the Promised Land. But her future was no less uncertain, and she was doing this alone. For the first time in her life, she had no family or friends to help her. Surely she wouldn't always find strangers as nice as the one in the post office. Would she be able to cope with whatever the future held?

Chapter Four

Avi introduced Esty to Noa and Gadi, and then apologised for having to leave so soon. In no time, Esty found herself sitting in another room with two more strangers. Both were relaxed and friendly, making Esty feel relatively comfortable. Noa seemed like the mothering type, with her well-stocked body, warm smile and soothing voice. Suddenly Esty's eyelids felt heavy and she realised she hadn't been listening to her hosts.

Noa noticed. "It's been a hard day for you, hasn't it?"

"It's the strangeness of everything. New people, new places, a new way of life. I'm sorry."

"That's all right. I'll show you to your room and in the morning you can meet the children, if you're awake before they go to school and kindergarten."

"I'm looking forward to that." Esty stood up, picked up her worldly belongings and followed Noa along a corridor of the large flat.

***

Esty rolled over and was surprised to be able to continue unhindered. Where was Chani's little body? Had she woken again, crying? Had Mum taken her to their bed again? Esty should have been there to comfort her. Mum shouldn't have been disturbed. Esty should try to wake up when Chani cried. Then she remembered.

A clock radio in the room showed half past five, the time she always woke to say her prayers and perform all her chores. Today, Friday, she would be especially busy helping her mother with the cleaning and cooking in preparation for the Sabbath.

For the first time since her escape, Esty thought of her parents and wondered how they were coping without her. They must be worried about her. She didn't think they'd have gone to the police. People always tried to keep any problems within the community. They didn't trust the authorities and didn't want secular police officers meddling in what they saw as their internal affairs. And they were even more afraid of anything getting to the non-haredi media.

The worry was understandable. A cousin of Esty's had once been accused of embezzlement. Much had been made, in the secular press, of the fact that he was a haredi. The articles gave the impression that their community was rife with criminals. Nothing could be further from the truth.

Would her parents realise why she'd disappeared? Esty thought they might have suspected the truth but that they might not discuss their ideas, even to each other, at this stage. She thought the most they'd do would be to put out some cautious feelers. And she decided she'd better phone them soon before their worries overcame their fears. Her escape was bound to cause her parents some embarrassment when family and friends asked after her. She didn't want to cause them any extra distress.

Then there was the kindergarten. Esty hated having to leave them in the lurch like that, but a new girl was coming to volunteer today. That was why Esty had chosen yesterday to make her escape. Esty should really have been there to show her the ropes, but she'd probably manage even without Esty's help.

Esty put on the clothes she'd arrived in to visit the bathroom. On her return, instead of saying her prayers as she normally would, she spoke to her reflection in the mirror on the inside of the wardrobe door. "Goodbye, Old Esty. This is where you take your leave."

As Esty watched, the image in the mirror slipped out of the long skirt and pulled off the long-sleeved top, stooping to stuff both garments into the bottom drawer of the empty wardrobe.

Then she emptied the contents of the plastic bag onto the bed and examined them. Two pairs of trousers and a few tops. And some underwear.

Of the trousers, one was a pair of jeans. Esty tried them on and immediately removed them, shocked. It wasn't that they didn't fit. On the contrary; they fitted too well, exactly following the curves of her body. And they only just covered her bottom. She couldn't possibly wear those.

She tried on the other pair – black, lighter material and looser fitting – but still gasped in horror. How could she?

The tops were short-sleeved or sleeveless with varying necklines. Esty chose a black, short-sleeved tee shirt with the word Mexico on the front. When she heard sounds outside her room, she opened the door cautiously, feeling only half-dressed.

Even more so when she peered round the door and saw two almost-naked children, who didn't seem at all embarrassed.

"Who are you?" they asked together, a little girl and a younger boy.

"I'm…." Esty stopped. Who was she indeed? A creature in metamorphosis, something between a caterpillar and a butterfly. Neither here nor there.

Noa came out of a bedroom carrying a baby who was wearing only a nappy. "Children, this is Esty. She's going to stay with us for a while. Now hurry up and get dressed."

As the children ambled off, Noa said, "Sorry for the commotion. Mornings are always like this."

"That's all right," said Esty. "I'm used to that." But really, she wasn't. Even though twelve of them squeezed into a small, two-bedroomed flat, mornings were better organised. They had to be; otherwise they'd turn into bedlam. Everyone knew what to do and they all got on with it. Esty's mother didn't have to remind anyone. Again Esty wondered who was doing her job today. Who was helping two-year-old Penina while her mother was occupied with the baby?

"Can I help?" Esty forced herself to leave her room, trying

25

her best to ignore her half-dressed state.

"Could you just remind Shirli and Roey to get a move on?" They tend to get... distracted." Noa returned to the room with the baby.

Esty found Shirli sitting on her bed in her underwear, totally absorbed in something on her lap. From the door, Esty could see what looked like the pink lid of an open box. As she got closer, she saw Shirli was frantically pressing buttons. She watched for a minute until Shirli suddenly stopped. "I lost."

"Lost what?"

"The game, stupid. What did you think I was doing?"

A mixture of shock and embarrassment flooded Esty for a moment. Then she pushed the feelings away, replacing them with the fruits of her experience with her younger siblings and the children in the kindergarten. "Shirli, we don't know each other yet and we don't have time to talk now. When we do, I hope you'll understand why the things I know are different from the things you know. But what I want to say to you now is that being different doesn't make me stupid. Do you understand?"

Shirli nodded.

"Good. Now, aren't you supposed to be getting dressed?"

"Oh yeah." Shirli put the instrument on the bed and picked up a pair of shorts.

Next door, Roey was playing with plastic soldiers. "Kya! Wham! Boom!"

Esty had to call his name three times before he looked up. When he did, the timidity written on his face, the inclination of the head to one side reminded Esty of the young man who had helped her in the post office. So strange how the face of a nameless, kind human being kept appearing in her mind. "I think you'd better get dressed," she said.

Another pair of shorts was grudgingly raised.

In the large kitchen, Noa was busy making sandwiches and hot chocolate drinks. "I'll drop off the kids," she said. "Then we can have a calm breakfast together. I don't work on Fridays."

"I wonder if I could use your phone while you're out. Just for a quick call."

"Yes, of course. Are you going to…?" A scream made Noa switch her attention. "Roey, that's Eliyor's chocolate biscuit. You've already eaten yours."

***

Eventually, the door closed behind the other four and Esty eyed the phone, nestled amongst piles of papers on a shelf in the hallway. This was her opportunity and she had to take it. She willed herself to pick it up and press the buttons.

"Hello?"

Her mother's voice. Esty had known her father wouldn't be at home at this time. He'd be studying at the yeshiva, swaying backwards and forwards, stroking his long beard in a room full of others doing the same. He wouldn't have missed this daily ritual just because his daughter was missing. On the contrary. He would believe that if he prayed and performed good deeds, God would help him to find her, showing him the words in the holy books that pointed to the solution to the mystery.

"Mum." Esty's voice was only a whisper. She repeated the word a little louder.

"Esty?" Her mother sounded relieved but worried at the same time. "What happened? Where are you?"

There was no way to soften the blow, or none that Esty could think of. "Mum, I'm sorry I couldn't tell you this before but… I've decided to leave the community. I want to be secular."

Silence.

"Mum?"

"I can't talk now. Call me later."

***

Noa returned to find Esty sitting at the kitchen table, sobbing quietly.

She sat down beside her and put an arm round her slim waist. "What happened?"

Esty dried her tears with the tissue she'd found in the kitchen. "I don't know what I expected, but it wasn't this. I told my mother what I've done and she put the phone down." Esty covered her face with her hands as the tears returned.

"I'm so sorry." Noa handed Esty another tissue. "Didn't she say anything at all?"

"She said, 'I can't talk now,'" said Esty between sobs. "Then she said, 'Call again later.' She sounded harsh – angry. Not at all like usual."

"Maybe there was someone else with her in the house. She wants to talk to you when she's alone."

Esty nodded and wiped her eyes. "You could be right. I didn't think of that."

Noa busied herself putting food and drinks on the table, refusing Esty's offer of help. "Not today. Today you can relax and get used to your new surroundings. But please stay here and talk to me. Tell me about your day yesterday – how you got out."

"It wasn't hard, really. I went to work in the kindergarten as usual. I had to try to forget what I was going to do. In the afternoon, instead of going home, I walked to the main post office to phone the organisation. Then I only had to follow Avi's instructions."

"How did you know the phone number?"

"A few months ago, I was walking in town when I passed someone I used to know. I called her name, but she kept on walking. I thought she hadn't heard me, so I ran after her and still she didn't stop, until eventually she turned down a side street and signed to me to follow her, and then we stopped in a doorway."

"Wow. What was she up to? It sounds like spy stuff."

28

Esty shook her head. "No, not at all. She did what I've just done and she was dead scared of meeting someone she knew before. Not only for her sake but theirs, too. She kept saying I should leave her alone, for my own good. But I stayed and in the end she told me the number to call and swore me to secrecy. She didn't want anyone to think she was causing others to leave the community."

"Anyway, that made it easy for you."

"It helped a lot, but there were a couple of problems."

"What were they?"

"Well.... On the way to the bus stop, I bumped into a woman I know. She started asking me questions and I was afraid she'd realise something was up. She must have seen that I was dying to get away from her. And before that, in the post office, I didn't know how to use the public phone."

"Oh dear. How did you manage?"

"I was lucky. A nice man let me use his mobile."

"How kind."

"Yes." Yet again, the man's image flashed through Esty's mind. The concern written on the slightly tilted, questioning face. "He even moved away and let me make the call in private." Esty smiled and let her eyes wander as she recalled the episode.

Noa raised her eyebrows.

"You know...." Esty stopped, wondering whether she was doing the right thing, but having started she felt she had to continue. "I don't know if I ought to say this, but you probably know it anyway. My teachers always said that secular people are bad. They said only we keep the commandments to help those in need, but secular people are selfish and care only about themselves."

"That doesn't surprise me. Did you believe that?"

"My friends did. They believed everything the teachers told us, but I found it hard. It seemed to me that even people who didn't believe in God would want to help other people simply because... well, if someone's in a bad state you want to help

29

them to feel better."

Noa nodded. "That's what I think. I don't need anyone to tell me to be helpful. If someone needs help and I can provide it, then I do."

"Well I definitely need help now and I'm very grateful that you're providing it."

Noa smiled.

"Everyone I've met so far on this journey has been kind. Avi and you and the man in the post office – even though he didn't know me at all."

Noa touched Esty's arm. "Be careful who you put your trust in. Not everyone on this side of the fence is kind. Some people appear to be kind, but really they want to get something out of you."

"I have to say that's true on the haredi side, too."

The phone rang and Noa went to answer it, returning soon afterwards. "That was my friend, Sarah. She invited us for lunch tomorrow at their place. You too."

"Thank you. Did you tell them who I am?"

"No. I wasn't sure if you wanted me to tell. I said we had a girl staying with us."

Esty sipped her lukewarm coffee. "Thanks. I think I'd rather not tell people straight away. I don't want them to think of me as a haredi person. They'd probably think I was weird and treat me differently."

"You might find that keeping your background secret is harder than you think," Noa warned.

"How do you mean?"

"You'd be surprised. You'll keep coming across things you don't know about. Computers, for instance. And television programmes. The news. Have you ever read a newspaper that's not haredi?"

Esty's teachers used to tell them what things were like in the secular world. They told the girls that newspapers and televisions showed bad things, like women with bare arms.

When the girls were older, the teachers said that television had sex on it. By that time, Esty had started to wonder how much of what they said was true, and whether they even knew the truth. Surely that act between a man and his wife was too intimate for anyone to show on a screen.

"I know it's going to be hard," Esty replied. "But I'll try to keep it hidden, at least when I first meet people."

As for what might happen when she got to know people better – well, that remained to be seen.

***

Towards evening, half an hour before the start of the Sabbath, when her parents were bound to have no visitors, Esty took a phone to her room, walking with slow ponderous steps. What if they didn't want to talk to her? What if they shunned her, went through the mourning procedure for her and never spoke to her again? What if she could never see her brothers and sisters again? What if she'd made a terrible mistake – one she'd regret all her life?

Chapter Five

Esty squeezed into the back of the car with the children, trying to ignore the voice inside her that was saying, *Honour the sabbath day and keep it holy.* That was all it needed to say, because she knew exactly what those words meant. Riding in a car on this special day of the week was strictly forbidden, or always had been up to now. In her neighbourhood, from sunset on Friday to sundown on Saturday, no vehicles could be seen or heard. People walked in the roads. The resulting calm, other-worldly atmosphere was part of what made this day so unique.

That voice had been very forceful over the past seventeen hours, reminding her of all the things she *should* or *shouldn't* be doing. It said she should pray, say blessings before doing anything, recite grace after meals, and she shouldn't turn on lights or any electrical equipment or eat anything that had just been cooked. The lists went on and on. She countered every item with the argument that she no longer believed in those things. Besides, there had been none of the usual signs of the Sabbath. No candles were lit, no wine drunk, no plaited bread eaten.

"That's how life is going to be from now on," she told the voice. "Get used to it." And the voice went quiet, as if it had given in and retreated. Before Esty went to bed, she gave herself an imaginary medal for bravery. But in the morning, the voice turned out to be more resourceful than she'd imagined. Its retreat had just been a temporary one, to allow itself to regroup. When she tore a piece of toilet paper from the roll, breaking the rule against tearing paper, put on the trousers – "men's clothes" – or pressed the switch on the kettle for coffee, the voice was back in full force, attacking her from all sides, filling her with doubts.

Where her parents were concerned, though, Esty was adamant. They'd been totally unreasonable and she wasn't going to cave in to their demands. If they continued to behave like that, she would have to get used to not having them in her life, as hard as that would be. Maybe she could find a way of meeting her brothers and sisters without her parents knowing. Surely they wouldn't be so stubborn.

Esty had panicked on realising she didn't have anything to wear for the lunch outing. Noa, studying her, had said, "I'm sorry, we don't have anything to fit you. We only have children's clothes and my clothes that would swamp you. But you don't have to worry. Everyone will be dressed informally. You can wear those clothes and tomorrow you can get some more." Esty had found another black short-sleeved top in the bag Liat had given her. Its neckline was a bit lower than the tee shirt's, but Esty tried not to think about that too much.

After a short journey, Gadi parked the car and the family and Esty trundled out and into a house with more children. Amidst considerable commotion as children ran all round them, Esty was introduced to the hosts and another family as a distant cousin. Then all the adults filtered into the living room, where Esty stopped in amazement. A long table was laid with a white tablecloth, cutlery, wine glasses, wine for the *kiddush* blessing and what looked like plaited loaves covered with a special cloth for the Sabbath.

Esty couldn't get to grips with this. She'd just left all this behind, said goodbye to it and decided to be secular. And Sarah and her family had looked secular. They were wearing secular clothes and didn't have their heads covered. So what was going on?

Noa must have seen Esty's surprise and confusion. "Don't worry," she whispered. "They're not orthodox – they're traditional."

Traditional. What did that mean? Just when Esty was getting

a taste of being secular, this other thing turned up.

Behind her, Esty heard someone else being introduced. She turned round and… gasped again.

"Esty, this is…" Noa began, then stopped and looked from one to the other. "Do you two know each other?"

Esty recovered before he did. "This is the man I mentioned – the one who was so kind to me at the post office."

***

Mark couldn't believe his eyes at first. It had to be that same girl – no doubt about it. The image of that face had been his constant companion for almost two whole days. And yet, in the post office, he'd been sure her garb marked her out as religious, while today she was dressed in trousers and a short-sleeved top. He didn't think he could have been mistaken on Thursday. It didn't make sense.

And now she was telling someone where they'd met. And smiling that gorgeous smile – the one that had appeared to him in his dreams. And the woman was saying, "Well, I'll let you two get to know each other properly."

Now the girl was saying something. Mark had to force himself to listen.

"What a coincidence! We'd better introduce ourselves. I'm Esty."

Mark's voice wouldn't come out at first. He cleared his throat. "Mark."

"Are you related to Sarah?"

Damn, thought Mark. *I should have shaken her hand. Too late now.* "Er… no. I only met her recently. It was very nice of them to ask me for lunch." Something prevented him from saying where he'd met them and made him hesitate even more than he usually did when speaking Hebrew.

"I noticed your accent. Shall we speak in English?" Esty asked in an almost English accent.

34

Mark relaxed at this opportunity to converse in his native tongue.

"Where do you come from?" Esty asked.

"London. How about you?"

"Me? Oh, I've always lived in Jerusalem but my grandparents live in London."

"You speak English very well."

"I speak to my mother in English. She taught me."

People were moving over to the table. Not the children. They were apparently being looked after in the kitchen. Mark and Esty found themselves standing behind adjacent chairs. After the blessings over the wine and bread, for which the men donned the traditional skullcaps, the guests all sat down and the hosts handed out chicken soup.

All through the meal, Esty plied Mark with questions and seemed very interested in what he had to say. He told her he'd been in Israel for almost a year, that he lived in a flat with three other new immigrants and was saving up for the deposit to buy a flat of his own. He told her about his job as a computer programmer.

"Why did you move to Israel?

"Various reasons. Perhaps the main one was that I wanted to be more independent. My parents had always overprotected me, but when I returned home after being away at university, I found it hard to live with them. They still treated me like a little boy. They wanted to know where I was all the time, and worried if I wasn't back exactly when I said I would be."

"That does sound hard."

"Do you live with your parents?"

"I... well, yes and no. I'm kind of in the process of moving away."

Mark wanted to ask more, but he didn't. Something told him he shouldn't, although he couldn't work out what that something was.

"Do you have any hobbies?" Esty asked as they started on the fruit salad.

Mark was glad he had an answer to that. "I've recently discovered Israeli folk dancing. I go every week, sometimes twice a week. It's great fun."

"That does sound fun. I like dancing."

"What sort of dancing do you do?"

"Oh nothing organised like that. But I like to dance at weddings and other functions."

"You should try folk dancing. You'd probably enjoy it."

"Well… maybe. I'll think about it."

Mark's heart leapt as Esty smiled yet again. He hadn't expected to see that smile ever again. And now here it was, along with the rest of this amazing girl.

"Where is it?"

"What? Oh the folk dancing." Mark blushed at his lapse in concentration. He gave Esty all the details. "I hope to see you there on Thursday."

Walking back home after the meal, Mark gave himself a slap on the thigh. What an idiot he was, blabbering on about where he came from, where he lived, his job and all that. He should have asked about her. He didn't have a clue about who she was apart from some vague comment about working with children.

And what had stopped him from saying where he'd met their hosts? It must have been the fact that it was connected to religion, and he was confused about where Esty stood on the religion issue. He thought again about the clothes Esty wore in the post office. Only an orthodox woman would wear such clothes in the summer. Unless she wanted to *appear* to be orthodox. But why on earth would Esty do that? There must be a lot about her that he didn't know. He really should have asked.

Mark went through what he remembered of their conversation. He really had, somehow, got the impression that she didn't want to say much about herself. It was probably rubbish. Didn't everyone like to talk about themselves?

She probably thought he was selfish and uncaring. It wasn't that at all. It was… shyness he supposed, a fear of being thought nosy. So stupid.

Later in the afternoon, Mark broached the topic with Claude. "You've been with a lot of girls, right?"

"Oh là là! Many, many girls, I cannot count." Claude held up his hands, fingers spread out.

"Did they usually like to tell you about themselves?"

"Oh yes! They are only happy when you ask them questions and show you are interested."

"Did you ever have a girlfriend who didn't want to talk about herself?"

"No – never."

Mark gave himself a silent rebuke. Idiot!

Chapter Six

"Right. Time for an afternoon nap," Noa announced as she entered the flat with the baby over her shoulder.

"But I'm not tired," Shirli whined. "You always make me go to bed when I'm not tired."

"I'm not tired either." Esty raised an eyebrow towards Noa and received a nod in return. "I know. You could show me your game – on the pink box."

"That pink box is a computer, stupid."

"Shirli!" Noa stared at her daughter. "That's no way to talk to our guest."

"Shirli." Esty's voice was quiet but firm. "Do you remember what I told you yesterday when you called me stupid?"

"You said you're not stupid. You're different. But you didn't tell me why you're different."

"All right, let's do a deal. You tell me about your game and I'll tell you why I'm different."

Shirli ran to her room. Esty exchanged grins with Noa before following Shirli and closing the bedroom door.

***

"So that's it," said Shirli. "Do you want to have a go?"

"Yes – thank you."

Honour the sab..., Esty heard. She gritted her teeth and refused to let the voice continue.

With Shirli's help, Esty managed to survive the game for a few moments before losing.

"Do you want to learn another game?"

"Do you have others?" Esty looked around for more pink

boxes.

"Of course. There are lots of games on this computer." Lots of games in one little pink box. What a strange world.

"Well, I think that's enough for today. You can teach me one another day."

"How come you don't know about computers?"

Esty pondered, wondering how she could explain to a six-year-old. "Where I grew up, it was actually quite near here, but it was so different you could think of it as another world."

"Like on another planet? Like Mars?"

"Yes. Let's say I was born on Mars."

"What was it like? Did you live in a flat like ours? Did you go to school? Did you have two silly little brothers?

"I lived in a flat, but it was much smaller than yours. We only had two bedrooms."

Shirli counted. "One for you, one for your parents. So where did your brothers sleep?"

"At the beginning, my parents slept in one room and I slept in the other, because I was the oldest – like you. But my mother kept having more babies. In the end, there were ten of us."

"Ten people in one little flat?"

"No – ten children."

"Ten children? Where did you all sleep?"

"The boys in one room, the girls in the other and our parents in the living room. It's still like that. Except I'm not there any more." Why did that make her sad?

"How many girls?"

"Seven."

"Seven children in one room?"

"We shared beds."

"Eugh! I couldn't sleep with someone else in the bed."

"You could if you had to. You'd get used to it. You'd get so used to it that you'd find it hard to sleep without someone else in your bed."

"Where did you put all your books and toys and things?"

39

"I didn't have many of those."

"Do all the mothers on Mars have lots of babies?"

"Yes. Some have even more than ten."

"There must be lots and lots of people on Mars."

"There are quite a lot."

"What else is different on Mars?"

"Lots of things. Girls all wear long skirts and long sleeves."

"All the time? Even in sports lessons?"

"We didn't have sports lessons."

"Wow. What else?"

"There are no televisions and not many computers."

"Why not?"

"Because the people think some of the things you see on them are bad."

"Like fighting and stuff?"

"Yes."

"But everyone knows the fighting's not real. It's all made up."

Esty shrugged her shoulders. It wasn't just the fighting. It wasn't just the men and women touching, either. It was seeing people who were different from them. It was seeing people behave in a way that was different from the way they believed people should behave.

Gnawing questions appeared in Esty's mind that had never been there before. If their way was the right way, why was it so bad for them to see the wrong way? Could it be that the rabbis were afraid that glimpsing the other world might make people want to join it? Surely if they were convinced that they were right and everyone else was wrong, they wouldn't be so afraid. Did the rabbis worry that people could be swayed to do bad things, like the Children of Israel who built the golden calf because they didn't have enough faith in God? Or were they themselves not confident enough that their way was right?

And what if denying yourself the pleasures of this life didn't help you to get to a good place in the next world? What if the next world didn't even exist? Then they would all have been missing the fun for absolutely no reason. And her father would have spent his life studying and praying for no reason. And her mother would have worked her fingers to the bone for no reason at all.

Perhaps she was judging that life too harshly. True, her mother worked very hard, as did all the mothers. And Esty often noticed a sad, wistful expression on her face, especially when those letters arrived from England. But she clearly loved her husband and children. She was devoted to them and delighted in everything they did. And after completing all the preparations for the Sabbath, when she lit the candles to welcome in the holy day, then she was at peace, joyful and serene.

That was the life they had intended for Esty – the life she had escaped from. Had she really left because she didn't agree with it? Or was it because she wasn't good enough for it – because she wouldn't have been able to cope with it? So many questions.

***

"Did you have a nice time at the lunch today?" Noa asked Esty later when they managed to snatch some time alone in the kitchen.

"Yes, very much. But I thought the religious part was very strange. I mean, they said the blessings for wine and bread but they didn't wash their hands in between. And they didn't say grace after the meal."

Noa was on her knees, loading the dishwasher. "That's what I meant by traditional. They keep some of the commandments but not all of them. They belong to a synagogue, but they go there by car."

"I didn't know there were people like that. I know there are orthodox people who aren't haredi, but I didn't think they would drive on the Sabbath."

"They don't – not the orthodox ones."

Esty frowned. "I do seem to have a lot to learn." She moved some dirty plates so that they'd be within Noa's reach.

"Thanks. I noticed you talking to Mark all the time."

"He's very nice." Esty felt her heart flutter as she spoke. "And he seemed to want to see me again. He said he does folk dancing and suggested I went, too."

"What a good idea. Will you go?"

"I'm not sure. I like dancing, but I'm only used to dancing with other women – at weddings, for instance."

"At weddings?"

"Yes – you know. On the women's side of the partition in the hall."

Noa frowned. "No, I don't know. You mean the men and women are completely separate, like in two different halls?"

"Almost. You can hear what's going on on the other side."

"So the women don't get to see the wedding?"

"Oh yes, they open up the partition for the ceremony so the women can see, and close it straight after."

"How strange."

Esty shrugged her shoulders. It had never seemed strange to her before, but for Noa clearly it was. Her thoughtful expression told Esty they were both learning about each other's worlds.

"Didn't you have any awkward moments when you were talking to Mark?"

"Yes, a few, but I managed to steer the conversation back to him each time. Fortunately he didn't make me say much about myself."

"What about other people?"

"Someone asked me how I'm related to you. I said it's so complicated and distant that I can't remember." Esty smiled.

"You know what?" Noa stopped loading and looked up at Esty for a moment. "I think you're going to make it through this transition. I think you have the right combination of determination and friendliness to get you there. Keep smiling like that and people will warm to you."

Esty smiled again, pleased that Noa had confidence in her. She didn't have quite so much confidence in herself, but determined to do her best to make Noa's prophecy come true.

Chapter Seven

As Esty climbed the steps, pushed open the door and entered the building, she was a mixture of excitement and apprehension, wanting to dance but afraid of encountering another new situation, looking forward to seeing Mark again but afraid he'd be turned off by something she did, in her ignorance of the norms in this new society.

The last five days had gone well. With Avi's help, there was a possibility of a job, starting in nearly three months at the end of August. An assistant kindergarten teacher had had to resign suddenly and it looked as if Esty would be chosen to replace her. There had been some talk about whether Esty's education fulfilled the requirements of twelve years of schooling. She'd learnt a lot about bible studies, religious observances and so on, but she hadn't learnt any maths or history or anything about the land she lived in, except where it related to bible stories. Avi had lent her some books and she'd been frantically trying to catch up before some kind of test she was to take soon.

All of this had happened through connections. Some relative of Avi's wife, Liat, knew the woman who ran the private kindergarten. Some practices were surprisingly similar to those of the world she'd grown up in. There, too, people got ahead through the people they knew. They even used the same word for it: *protectsiya*.

Noa had taken her clothes-shopping in the local Malcha shopping centre, which happened to be *the* shopping centre of Jerusalem. That had been very embarrassing – changing in a cubicle with only a curtain between her almost-naked body and other people, some of them men. Then she'd had to come out to look at the mirror and for Noa to see.

Esty had visited the shopping centre before, but not to buy clothes. They'd looked at the clothes in the shop windows, but only bought equipment and utensils, and they always kept their purchases down to a minimum. When they needed new clothes, they went to a local shop, where men didn't enter and changing cubicles had doors that locked.

Noa hadn't managed to persuade Esty to buy anything brightly coloured or sleeveless or low-necked or tight fitting. "You have such a perfect body," she'd said looking envious. "Why don't you make the most of it?" "I couldn't," Esty had replied. "Not yet." Would she ever get used to those tight, revealing clothes? She wasn't sure. Perhaps feeling able to wear them would be a sign that she had made it to the other side.

Then Esty had accompanied Noa to the supermarket on the ground floor. Esty knew the way. It was strange how the shopping centre looked familiar but different, as if she were looking at a wall for the first time from the other side. There were the same three floors of shops, most of them quite small. The same crowds thronging the passageways. The same noise from said crowds. The same mix of people, from haredi to secular, all identifiable by the clothes they were wearing.

While going down on the escalator, Esty had spotted Mrs Greenspan with another woman she recognised. Fortunately, Esty had been standing on the far side from the women. She immediately hid behind Noa and was pretty sure the two women, locked in conversation, hadn't spotted her. But Noa had noticed her confusion. "What's up?" "Just some people from my past," Esty had replied, warming to the comforting hug from Noa and her promise. "It'll get easier."

Esty had also written to her grandparents in London. That hadn't been easy, as she'd never had any connection with them before. It was perfectly possible that they wouldn't want to know her at all. She wrote something about that.

My mother often mentions you with fondness when she tells

45

stories from her childhood. But she never talks about you now – since she left home and came to live in Israel. It's almost as if you don't exist any more. I know you do, though, because I've seen the envelopes with your address written on them.

I expect you don't want to know me, but I thought I'd write to find out. I hope you don't mind.

"Is there folk dancing going on here this evening?" Esty asked the guard at the entrance.

"Yes. Down there." With his head, the guard indicated the stairs.

Taking a few deep breaths, Esty descended the stairs towards the unknown. When would she be able to do these things without worrying? She paid the entrance fee to the girl sitting at a table and went in.

The hall was large and had strange wooden bars on the walls. The markings on the floor looked familiar, and Esty realised this hall must double as a hall for playing that basketball game she'd seen on Noa's and Gadi's television. A few people were seated on benches alongside the bars.

Behind a table, a man was fiddling with electronic equipment. Esty approached him. "Hello, I'm new."

The man sounded pleasant enough. "Welcome. I'm Baruch." He held out his hand.

Esty forced her hand to meet his, hoping he wouldn't notice her diffidence.

"We'll start in a few minutes," said Baruch, adding, "Don't worry. Everyone is a beginner. Even me."

Baruch grinned and Esty grinned back, despite everything.

As soon as she sat down, Esty saw Mark coming towards her, smiling. "I'm so glad you came," he said. "You seemed unsure when I mentioned it. It's great fun, really. I'm sure you'll like it."

Then Baruch appeared in the centre of the room and they all formed a circle round him. Baruch explained and demonstrated, and Esty picked up the steps quickly. It wasn't very different from the dances she'd learnt at school, the same ones she'd enjoyed dancing in the women's section at weddings and bar-mitzvah parties. The main difference here was that there were also men in the circle. When Baruch turned on the music, he told them to hold hands. Fortunately, Esty was standing between two women.

After learning a few dances and starting to feel more relaxed, Esty was startled by Baruch's instruction to form couples and Mark's sudden appearance beside her.

"Will you dance with me?"

Her heart thumping, Esty nodded and took her place beside Mark on the outside of the circle. Baruch held his partner's hand and Mark did the same with Esty. Mark's hand felt large, his grip firm. Despite her discomfort, Esty also felt a tingle inside that wasn't completely unpleasant. As before, Baruch explained and demonstrated. Esty followed, feeling much more tense than before. Then she found she had to put her arms round Mark's shoulders while Mark hugged her waist, and she froze.

"Don't worry. Relax. It doesn't matter if you make a mistake," said Mark, apparently misunderstanding the reason why she was holding back.

Esty forced herself to perform the actions required of her, and somehow managed to continue to the end of the dance. But it was enough. She couldn't face any more couple dancing. She said, "Thank you," and went to sit down on a bench.

Esty stayed to watch, enjoying the music, the dancing and the happy atmosphere. An older woman spoke to her. "Are you new? I haven't seen you here before."

"Yes. It's my first time."

"Really? You dance very well – I noticed. I hope you keep coming."

"I think I will," Esty replied. And she meant it. She turned back to watch the dancers. Yes. This was an activity she could see herself doing and enjoying. In time, she told herself, she would even get used to the couple dancing.

When she decided to leave, Esty looked around for Mark to say goodbye to him and was surprised not to see him anywhere.

***

Mark watched as Esty left him. He saw her make straight for a bench and sit down next to an older woman. What had he done wrong? Why did Esty find him so repulsive that she couldn't bear to carry on dancing with him?

No longer having a partner, Mark sat down, too. He chose a bench on the opposite side of the hall from where Esty had gone. Obviously she wanted nothing to do with him. When the hall started to fill up as the more advanced dancers appeared, Mark crept out and vanished into the night.

For an hour or two Mark wandered, not taking much notice of where he was. At one point, a familiar ringing sound suddenly woke him up to the fact that he was standing on the light railway track in Jaffa Road and he'd better get off it before the train arrived. Apart from that, he roamed the streets in a daze, ignoring the crowds around him. When he found himself outside his block of flats, he hoped to be able to reach his room without anyone seeing him, but Claude was there in the living room.

"Hey, Mark, what's up? You look… *misérable*."

"I'm okay." Mark tried to escape to his room.

"Tell me. It's a girl. *D'accord?*"

Mark sat down on the chair next to Claude. "I made a mistake, Claude. I thought she liked me, but she doesn't."

"How you know?"

"She danced one dance with me, and then she just went off."

"Maybe she go to the loo, or she go home."

"No." Mark shook his head slowly, in his mind seeing the beautiful and unattainable Esty sitting calmly on the bench, chatting happily with one of the women. He stood up and went

48

towards his room.

"Never mind," Claude called after him. "How you say? There are more fish in the sea?"

But none for me, thought Mark.

Chapter Eight

"You're lucky you get on with people so well," Noa said. They were sitting in the kitchen. Esty had just put the children to bed while Noa cleared up.

Esty took a sip of tea. "I don't try to make anyone like me. I'm simply interested in people, so I ask questions."

"And who isn't flattered by genuine interest?"

"Talking also helps me to learn about all the things I never knew – that and television. Do you know, I was watching a children's programme with Shirli today and it showed three children who needed to get to a place called Canberra. I said, I wonder where Canberra is, and Shirli said, 'Oh, it's the capital of Australia.' Just like that – without even thinking about it. When I asked her how she knew, she said it came up in a computer game. I hadn't realised children learn lots of things from games and television. I'm beginning to understand how much I've missed."

"There must be plenty of things you know that most people don't know."

"Hmm. That's true, but I wonder if any of it has any use on this side of the fence."

Koren, the kindergarten teacher, had also noticed gaps in Esty's knowledge when she interviewed her. Esty didn't even know any of the songs they sang. But Koren was impressed with Esty's knowledge of bible stories, and it was clear that Esty had a good relationship with all the young children with whom she'd come in contact. And besides, Koren and Esty got on well together, and Koren always felt it was important for the person she had to interact with day in and day out to be likeable. She'd heard about a nearby kindergarten where the teacher and her assistant were always arguing, and she didn't want her work environment to be like that. Besides upsetting the two women, the ill feeling between them also affected the children, making them fretful.

Koren's impression was that Esty's enthusiasm would enhance the happy atmosphere in her kindergarten, and that she would willingly carry out the necessary mundane tasks as well as the more interesting ones. As she told Esty, "I feel these two qualities outweigh your lack of knowledge." So Koren offered Esty the job on the spot – on a provisional basis. "But make sure you learn those songs," she'd said as they parted.

"You are settling down, aren't you – getting used to this life?" Noa asked cautiously.

"Yes, everything has gone well so far. Why do you ask?"

"Because there are moments you seem sad – as if something is missing – something you're sorry about. Is it the contact with your family?"

Esty nodded. "I do miss them – all of them. My parents and all my brothers and sisters."

"Are you sure there's no way you can meet them?"

Esty shook her head, feeling her ponytail bobbing from side to side. "No. They won't budge on that."

Noa inclined her head and peered into Esty's eyes. "What a shame. Perhaps they'll change their minds soon. I'm sure they miss you, too."

"Perhaps." Esty wasn't at all sure.

"Is anything else troubling you?"

"Well…."

"Tell me. I have broad shoulders." Noa grinned as she laid her hands on her shoulders to emphasise their size.

"It's about Mark."

"You two really hit it off together, didn't you?"

"I thought we did."

"But…?"

"I hoped he'd contact me. I…. It sounds ungrateful to say

this with so much going on and you've all been wonderful to me and I hardly know him, but... I miss Mark. I really liked him and I was hoping he'd also become a part of my new life, but I guess I was wrong and he isn't interested in me."

***

Mark dragged himself to the synagogue for the Saturday morning service. The previous week he'd stayed at home, too exhausted from putting on a show of normalcy at work every day. He'd skipped folk dancing, too. Then he'd given himself a good talking to. *Forget her. She's too good for you. She's not interested in you. Carry on as before and pretend you never met her.*

Sarah came over to him after the service. "Have you seen any more of Esty? I noticed how you two bonded at my place."

"No. I don't think she's interested in me."

"That's not what I heard. Noa says Esty's really hoping you'll get in touch. Do you have her phone number?"

***

It was Saturday evening by the time Mark picked up his phone and punched in the number. He was still riddled with doubts. What if Sarah had been wrong? What if Esty didn't want to see him?

Hearing her voice allayed his worries. She sounded delighted to hear from him. As he listened to her, he could imagine that smile and longed to see it again.

"There's an interesting film on at the Jerusalem Theatre. It's set in Afghanistan. Would you like to see it with me?"

"Yes – thank you."

"I thought we could have a meal there before the film."

"That sounds lovely."

"I'll see you at the theatre tomorrow at half past seven?"

As they said their goodbyes and hung up, Mark could hardly

believe it. Esty wanted to see him. She had agreed to go out with him.

Five minutes later, Esty phoned back and Mark feared she'd changed her mind.

"Mark, could we meet earlier – say a quarter to seven, at a different place, and then walk to the theatre?"

"Yes." Mark was surprised but had no objection.

"I want to meet in the area off the little road that goes down from the top of Yemin Moshe, by the windmill, towards the Lion Fountain. Do you know it?"

"Yes, but...."

"I'll tell you why when I see you."

***

When Claude returned home, he found Mark sitting at the table, an empty plate in front of him. In fact, Mark had finished that meal some time before, but had remained seated.

"Mark, you think too much, you know? Life is too short to think so much."

Mark sighed. "But sometimes life is complicated. You have to think about it."

"You want to talk instead?"

"Are you sure you want to listen?"

"I tell you what. You make tea and I listen."

Mark smiled. "You're on."

"On? On what?"

"Never mind. It's just an expression."

***

Claude was waiting at the table when Mark carefully carried in two full mugs, placing one in front of Claude and the chipped one where he sat down opposite Claude.

Claude sipped and gave a satisfied sigh. "It's good. With a

53

soupçon of lemon." He looked across at Mark's tea with its *soupçon* of milk and curled his upper lip. "How you drink that? It is the colour of washing dishes."

Mark smiled at their familiar tiff. "Oh no. It's the mark of good tea."

"Or the tea of Mark?" Claude set his mug on the table. "Okay, talk."

"The good news is, that girl I mentioned, the one I thought didn't want to know me, she wants to see me. We're going out for a meal and a film tomorrow."

"You see? I tell you she want you and I am right."

Mark wasn't so sure that was true. He remembered Claude talking about other fish.

"And the bad news?"

"Not bad exactly. Just strange. You know the windmill at Yemin Moshe?"

"What is windmill?"

"It's a tall round stone building with blades at the top that turn." Mark accompanied his words with hand signs to get his meaning across.

"*Le moulin*! Of course I know. Everyone know it. And it is very near to here. It is built in the nineteenth century by Sir Moses Montefiore, one of your British *philanthropes*. But it never work because they forget there is not sufficient wind."

"Actually I heard a different explanation in London."

"What explanation?"

"One Sunday morning, when I was still living there, I decided to join a tour of the Jewish East End. They pointed out the places where the Jews lived, worked and prayed when the East End was mostly Jewish."

"You become a tourist in your city?"

"Yes, I don't know why I went. I guess before leaving Britain I wanted to find out more about my roots. My grandfather was born in the East End and grew up there, but he died when I was little and I never heard much about his early life."

"What about the *moulin*?"

"I'm getting to that. The guide pointed out lots of landmarks and told us about their history. Then, towards the end of the tour, she took us to the Bevis Marks Synagogue, which still exists, and another guide showed us the seat that used to belong to Sir Moses Montefiore. He mentioned that Montefiore travelled the world starting various projects and providing funding – giving money – for them."

"Yes?"

"One of those projects was the whole neighbourhood of Yemin Moshe. It was one of the first neighbourhoods built outside the city walls, and it was named after him. Moshe is Hebrew for Moses."

"Yes, yes, I know this."

Mark took another sip of tea. "Okay, so this is the story. Moses Montefiore often travelled to the Holy Land, even though travel was hard in those days and he was getting old. On one of his visits, the residents of Yemin Moshe told him they were having problems getting flour. There were enough flour mills in the area, but they had all hiked up their prices and the people could no longer afford to buy flour from them. Montefiore announced that he would build several windmills to grind flour and that he would give away the flour to the residents. He had the first one built in Yemin Moshe. The mill began to work, the people received free flour and the other flour mill owners panicked and reduced their prices. This was what Montefiore had wanted. He didn't need to build any more windmills and the one he did build wasn't needed any more."

"Ha ha, I like this story. It's what you call 'win-win'."

"Exactly. Old Sir Moses must have been a very clever man."

"What is the link between the *moulin* and your girl?"

"She wants to meet me there."

"Why?"

"She wouldn't say. We're going to meet there and walk to the Jerusalem Theatre."

"It is close."

"I know. I don't mind doing it, but I don't understand why she wants to meet there."

"It is *mystérieux*. You must wait for tomorrow to discover the truth."

Chapter Nine

Meeting at quarter to seven meant that Mark had to rush home from work for a quick shower and change of clothes before hurrying out. Work had been annoying, as it often was on Sundays. After all these months, his internal clock still hadn't accepted the fact that Sunday was a workday. It didn't help that he had Fridays off instead. Sunday was Sunday.

Fortunately the shower was free and he managed to arrive at the agreed place just on time and exactly when Esty did, her radiant smile contrasting with her usual black clothes. Mark noticed that sunglasses hid her pretty eyes, even though the sun was going down by then.

After they greeted each other, Mark followed Esty to the railings, where the vista took in the Old City walls, and beside them the Valley of Hinnom with the hills behind and the distant hills that he knew lay on the other side of the Dead Sea, in Jordan. The valley was a rugged brown now, but Mark remembered the greens of winter. The views here were spectacular – one of the advantages to living in a hilly city, full of history. Towers and steeples poked up from behind the city walls and beside them. The Tower of David, the Dormition Abbey just outside, as well as two church steeples inside the walls. Modernity also towered behind the walls in the form of a tall aerial. Despite the aesthetically displeasing nature of the aerial, Mark loved this mixture of old and new. To the right, stood the old Church of St Andrew with its blue and white Scottish flag. The "old" here was comparative. It looked old when you got up close, with its partly blackened, mildewy bricks, but Mark knew it was still under a hundred years old – nothing compared to the almost six hundred-year-old city walls.

As they stood there, Mark could see the effects of the setting sun. The sun went down so much faster than it did in England that you could stand and watch as the changing light from behind caused the colours all over the vast panorama to dance as they grew darker.

Mark took in all of this with half his mind. The other half was waiting for the solution to the mystery. He felt impatient but decided not to ask. No doubt Esty would explain in her own time.

Then she began. "I need to tell you why I wanted us to meet here." The expression on Esty's face had become serious. "This was the place I came to on my last date. And the one before that."

Mark shifted his position, widening the gap between them a little. Why on earth was she telling him this?

Esty must have sensed his growing unease. "Wait. Please. There's more."

"I'm not sure I want to hear it."

Esty turned to face him, lips apart. "Why ever not?"

Could Esty really be as shocked as she looked? Mark didn't think so. Surely she realised that what she said could upset him. But she'd asked him to explain and, whether or not her question was as naïve as it sounded, he would attempt to spell it out to her.

"Well, to tell you the truth, what you just said makes me rather annoyed. What are you trying to tell me? That you brought your exes here when you wanted to break it off with them, and that you expect the same to happen with me, or you're even going to say goodbye to me now when we hardly know each other? Or that you want to return to one of them and you're merely using me as a substitute in the meantime?"

Esty shook her head. "I'm sorry. I'm not doing this well, but I need to tell you something and I thought this would be the best place. Please, Mark, listen to what I have to say." Her eyes implored him to give her a chance.

"All right." Mark made no move to close the gap between them.

"Don't look too obviously, but can you see those couples sitting on the benches behind us?"

Mark turned to look while Esty continued to look the other way. He saw three haredi couples sitting and talking. Each couple took up a whole bench because of the gap the boy and girl left between them. Then he turned back, perplexed. "Yes, I see them. What about them?"

"Do you see how they're sitting far enough apart so that there's no chance they'll touch each other by mistake?"

"Yes," Mark repeated, still not understanding where this was leading.

"All of those couples were introduced by a matchmaker. They came to this place to talk and see if they get on together. They might meet two or three times altogether. Then they have to make a decision. Either they decide to get married or they ask the matchmaker to introduce them to other potential partners."

"How do you know...?" The question stuck in Mark's throat. The truth was beginning to seep through the fog.

Esty clutched the railings as if she needed their support. "I was one of those. I sat on one of those benches, or on the steps leading down from the windmill, and talked to the man next to me. He was dressed in a black suit and hat, and had a beard and sidecurls. He talked about his world view and related everything he said to verses from the holy books."

"Which man?"

"Both of them. They were exactly the same. And the others I met before them. Well, not exactly, but they wore the same clothes and had the same thoughts. They wanted to know if I agreed with them and I... I lied, because what they said was what I was supposed to believe. I thought if I tried hard enough I would believe, and then I'd be what my parents wanted me to be – a good girl."

Mark kept silent; his brain was working hard to fit random

thoughts together like a jigsaw. Her clothes on that first meeting, the barrier he'd felt between them at the meal, despite her friendliness. At folk dancing, too, he remembered the way she'd held back.

"When it came to having to decide on a husband," Esty went on, "I couldn't do it. All I could see was my life stretching out in front of me, working, cleaning, cooking while my husband studied day and night. Getting pregnant every year. Never having time or money to enjoy myself. Never being allowed to do all sorts of things."

Esty turned to Mark and raised her eyebrows, as if requesting his permission to continue. He gave a slight nod.

"Every time they made me decide, I said no. I gave some excuse. He was too short, he stammered… anything. I even said about one of them that he wasn't pious enough. I knew I didn't want any of them. They put more and more pressure on me."

"Who did?"

"My parents, the matchmaker, my sisters, friends… everyone. Eventually I realised the only way out was to escape. So one day I did."

"When was that?"

"The day you saw me in the post office."

They were silent for a while as they leaned on the railings, oblivious to the sounds of people around them.

Mark was the first to break the silence. "When I saw you that day, I thought you must be orthodox. Not haredi – I didn't think of that – but orthodox, yes. Then when we met at the lunch you were wearing trousers. I couldn't make it out. I thought I'd made a mistake."

Esty smiled for the first time since she'd started her revelation, giving Mark hope that she was pleased with his reaction. "I felt so strange in trousers that day – as if I was almost naked."

"You hid it very well."

"I had to. I didn't want anyone to know."

"Why not?"

"I want people to see me as a person like any other. Not as a weird ex-haredi. But it was hard. I was pleased you didn't try to shake my hand on that day. I wasn't ready for that."

"And I was cross with myself for missing the opportunity. I was worried you'd think I was strange for not doing it."

Esty shook her head and smiled. When would she remove the sunglasses and let him see those beautiful eyes again?

"So why are you telling me all this now?"

"Because I'm not ready for what you might want to do with me – hugging and kissing and all that?"

"I'll take it slowly then. I'll wait till you're ready." Inside, Mark heaved a sigh of relief. As much as he longed to hold Esty in his arms, he was afraid his lack of experience would show when he tried.

Mark glanced at his watch. "We'd better start walking to the theatre now."

They walked in silence at first, each absorbed in their own thoughts. Then, as if continuing a conversation, Esty said, "That's why I didn't carry on dancing with you."

Mark turned to her. She had finally removed her sunglasses, restoring her lovely face to perfection. "Why?"

"Because I've been brought up in a world where men and women don't touch each other until they're married. I found it hard enough to hold your hand, but when I felt your hands on my waist it was too much for me. I'm sorry. I've spent my life doing things in a certain way. I can't change overnight."

"I thought it was me. I thought you didn't like me."

"Oh no – far from it."

***

Mark had been worried they wouldn't have enough to talk about during the meal, but after Esty's revelation the conversation flowed smoothly. In answer to a question from

Mark, Esty told him about her escape and everything that had happened since.

"Don't you want to have children?" Mark asked.

"I do – very much. Why did you think I don't?"

Mark was heartened by Esty's answer, although he wasn't sure why it should make such a difference to him. "You sounded worried about getting pregnant."

"No. I'm not worried about that, but I don't want to get pregnant every year. I want to have two or three children. I want to have time to love my children and to nurture them, to give them the best possible start in life. My mother never had enough time for me. There were always younger children who needed her more."

"How do your parents feel now? About you escaping like that?"

Mark saw a look he hadn't seen before on Esty's face – of determination, defiance maybe.

"I phoned them the day after I left. I spoke to them twice. The first time my mother answered but she couldn't talk to me. There might have been someone else there. The second time my father answered. He sounded furious. I've never heard him so angry before. It was…." The defiant look faded as tears appeared in her blue eyes. "It was hard to talk to him in that mood. I had to force myself to ask if we could meet."

Esty took a tissue out of her bag and blew her nose. Mark longed to hold her hand to soothe her.

"Did he agree to see you?"

"Yes. But only in a secret place and I was to dress in my old clothes."

"So you did meet them?"

"No. I couldn't agree to that. They have to accept me as I am now before I'll meet them."

"Preconditions. It sounds like political negotiations."

"How do you mean?"

"You know, when enemies agree to meet, or leaders of

different political parties work together to form a coalition."

"Actually, I don't know much about that. I was never encouraged to read newspapers or listen to the news."

"Perhaps you're better off not knowing. Most of the news items are downright depressing. Esty, you don't have to listen to me, but in my experience it's good to compromise."

"How do you mean?" Esty asked again.

"I think your parents have given up something by agreeing to meet you. Maybe you could compromise your principles a little by agreeing to their terms."

***

In the film, a scene showing an unpaved road, mud huts and women covered from head to toe, against a backdrop of mountains covered in a haze, gave way to the inside of a house, where a teenage girl was being instructed by her devout parents. It soon became clear that they were forcing her to marry a man three times her age, a man she hated. Esty sobbed quietly next to Mark.

"Do you want to leave?" he asked softly.

"No."

Instinctively, Mark placed his hand on Esty's thigh, then removed it. His heart leapt when she turned to him and smiled through her tears. He put his hand back on her thigh and kept it there.

Chapter Ten

"This is it," said Noa, stopping the car.

Esty grabbed the strap of her bag, remembering the note she'd put inside it. "Thank you so much for bringing me. I'd have felt stupid going around in these clothes."

"No problem. I'll be back in an hour."

Avi had helped to find the room, close to the town centre, in the home of another volunteer. The location would suit her parents – within walking distance but far enough away from prying eyes.

A woman opened the door for her. She was dressed in a skirt and a long-sleeved top, and Esty wondered if she'd dressed that way on purpose to appease her parents.

"I'm Esty."

The woman indicated the room. "Let yourselves out when you've finished."

Esty managed to say, "Thank you," before the woman followed her to the door of the room and closed it, leaving Esty alone with her thoughts. She sat down on an armchair feeling confused. She was about to see her own parents. The parents she had always loved, respected and honoured. So why did she now feel as if some terrible ordeal awaited her? Then she thought of the poor Afghan girl in the film she'd seen with Mark. That girl's parents had frightened her at the mere suggestion that she might not want to marry the man they had chosen for her. Later, there had been violence. Esty was shocked that such things could happen. She knew her father would never resort to violence against her, and yet her memories of the film made her more worried.

Esty had no idea what form this meeting would take, but she

had tried to prepare for it by listing possible questions and her answers. She would tell them why she left so that they'd understand. She would describe the family she was living with, so that they could be assured that she was being well looked after. Then she might talk about her plans for the future. And of course she would ask after them and all her siblings.

It wasn't long before the doorbell rang and the door to the room opened. Esty heard her mother's voice saying, "Thank you," and she stood up. Then her parents were in the room and her mother rushed to hug her. "Esty, darling."

Esty hugged her mother back. So they weren't angry. It was going to be all right after all. Then she looked up at her father and instantly changed her mind. She'd never seen him looking so stern, so angry. He didn't even say anything at first. He sat down on an armchair and cast a deep gloom around the room. The women sat down, too. Rivka took the other armchair and Esty sat on the edge of the sofa, too anxious to lean back.

In eerie silence, Esty observed her father, seeing him with new eyes. He didn't remove his black jacket, which, she knew, covered a long-sleeved white shirt, which in turn covered the fringed garment he always wore, its tassels hanging outside his trousers. This garb had always seemed normal to her. All the men she knew wore it. Now it seemed strange. It belonged to the other world that was no longer hers. And it was absurd to wear so much in this hot Middle Eastern climate. The room wasn't air-conditioned and he must have been sweltering in those clothes – more so in his current mood.

It seemed like an age before he spoke, his smouldering voice barely recognisable. "Why did you do this?"

Esty was ready for that, but she hadn't anticipated the atmosphere in which she'd be forced to give her answer. Struggling to keep her voice steady and to remember her lines, she said, "I felt I couldn't stay. I knew it wasn't the life I wanted. I couldn't believe in it."

"You, you, you! Did I really conceive such a selfish child?

Did I not teach you to care for others? To be charitable?" He had raised his voice. He sounded even more frightening.

"I do help others. But this was my decision, just for me. It has nothing to do with anyone else."

"So you're stupid as well as selfish. Very stupid."

Esty frowned, trying to make sense of her father's words. Someone else had called her stupid recently. Someone in the new world... the dream world. Did that world really exist? This was reality.

"Your sister's engagement has been called off. Your brothers and sisters are being taunted for having such a sister. Our whole family is being spurned by the community."

Still Esty remained silent. In fact the whole room was now so quiet and eerie that a passing car sounded like a juggernaut lorry. It was hard to tell how much time passed, but it felt awfully long. Esty spent it looking down at her skirt, unable to look either of her parents in the eye.

"Do you have anything to say for yourself?"

"I'm so sorry. I didn't think...."

"No. You were very naïve. And very selfish. Now you will have to live with what you have done. May God forgive you."

"Is there anything I can do to make things better for you?"

"No. It's too late for that now. You should have thought of that before. Go and live your life amongst the infidels. I won't break off contact with you completely, but I request that you do not try to contact your brothers and sisters. You have already made things very hard for them. You have confused them when most of them are too young to understand. Do not upset them further by talking to them."

Her father stood up to go and her mother followed.

"Wait!" Esty remembered the note in her bag and took it out. "This is my current address and phone number in case... in case you need to know."

The expression on her mother's face as she reached for the note didn't reflect her father's anger. Instead it showed sorrow and something else. Love? Yes, Esty thought so. At least, she hoped so.

Then they were gone and Esty had more than half an hour to sit and ponder. She sat down again and gave in to the tears she'd been holding back. As the tears flowed out, the reality of her father's words flowed in. She really was a bad girl. Selfish. Yes, extremely selfish. No consideration for anyone but herself. Why had she done it? How could she have done such an awful thing to the people she loved the most?

The more she thought, the more she saw what a hopeless position she was in. She couldn't go on and she couldn't go back. She was stuck and slowly sinking into a vicious quagmire.

Esty had no idea how much time had passed until she looked down at her watch again and gradually made sense of what the hands were telling her. Ten to eight. In ten minutes – or maybe earlier – Noa would be here to collect her. Noa. What could she understand? Noa thought Esty was a good girl. She kept saying so. But she was wrong. Esty was a very, very bad girl. And she had to get away quickly. Away from all the people who didn't know what a bad girl she really was.

Esty left the place and started walking, not caring where she was or in which direction her feet were taking her. Nothing mattered any more. She had to keep walking. Walking and talking. If she stopped, it would be the end of... the end of.... No, not the end – that would be far too easy. First, suffering. On earth. Lots and lots of suffering. Must suffer. Mustn't end it now. Too easy. Naughty. Bad. Wicked. The words echoed in her head as her footsteps echoed on the pavement. Evil. Selfish. Keep walking. Thoughtless... greedy... bad... bad... bad....

Chapter Eleven

Mark was almost home. He'd stayed later at folk dancing than he usually did. Sometimes it was such fun he didn't feel like leaving. This evening, he'd found a woman to dance with. They'd even chatted easily between dances. Baruch, the instructor, had been his usual lively self and this time Mark had actually understood most of his jokes.

It was about midnight when Mark left. He could have caught the last bus home but preferred to walk. And think. It was a shame Esty couldn't be there today. That would have made a great evening perfect. But she was meeting her parents and by the time the meeting finished she'd have missed the dancing for beginners. Besides, she'd said she probably wouldn't be in the mood for dancing after the meeting. He could understand that.

The walk brought Mark into Emek Refa'im Street. Valley of Ghosts Street. Some of Jerusalem's streets had such picturesque names, he thought. Like Dor Dor Vedorshav – Every Generation and its Demands. What was that about? He really ought to find out the origin of…. Something alerted Mark to the scene in front of him.

The street, even at this late hour, was full of young people going in and out of the cafés or hanging around outside. This area was well known as the place for youngsters to hang out, and this evening was the start of the weekend.

What was unusual was the orthodox girl weaving between the people. Well, not so much weaving as bumping into them all and continuing, as if she had no notion of their presence. She seemed to be muttering all the time. No – shouting. As she got closer to Mark, he recognised the bag, the skirt and then the face. "Esty!"

His voice made her turn suddenly to walk back, away from him, but she lost her footing and fell on the pavement. Mark rushed to her. "Esty. Are you all right?" He was shocked at her response.

"Keep away from me. Don't touch me. I'm evil. You must stay away from me, for your own sake." She was screaming. Tears streamed down her face. "Don't touch me!" she screamed even louder.

Something told Mark not to listen as Esty pleaded with him to keep his hands off her. Not this time. He knelt down beside her and held her arms down by her sides. She struggled. It struck him that he hardly felt her resistance.

"Esty, this is Mark. You're safe now."

Mark didn't know if Esty had heard him. His words hadn't made any difference. She was still screaming and crying. And making feeble attempts to free herself.

People were watching, of course. A few young guys approached and asked if he needed help. One of them explained. "We saw her going along the road like some crazy thing. And you know her?"

"Yes. She's not usually like this."

"Shall I call for an ambulance?"

"No." They'd treat her like a mental case, and she wasn't. She was Esty, sweet and kind. "Could you hold her for a minute while I make a phone call?" It occurred to Mark that she wouldn't normally want to be touched by strange men, but this was an emergency. And besides, Esty didn't seem to understand what was going on.

He took his phone from his pocket and managed to press the right buttons while keeping an eye on the scene beside him. What a relief to hear the soft French accent. "Claude, something's happened. I need you to come to Emek Refa'im Street. Now."

"But, *mon ami*, I have a girl...."

"I don't care. This is an emergency. Please Claude, I need you. I need you more than I've ever needed anyone before."

***

Claude and Mark were sitting drinking tea at the dining table. Esty, after more screaming and feeble attempts to escape, had fallen asleep on Mark's bed. The other two roommates, having woken up and complained, were back in their rooms. Claude's girl had left in disgust.

"I'm sorry about the girl," said Mark.

"No *problème*." Claude shook his index finger from side to side. "She is not... *spéciale*."

Mark sipped his tea in silence."

"What happen?"

"I don't know. I wasn't with her. I know she met her parents earlier this evening, for the first time since leaving them. I don't know what happened after that. I saw her by chance when I came home tonight."

"No, *mon ami*, there is no chance. Everything happen for a reason."

"Well, at any rate, I'm glad I was there. I dread to think what would have happened to Esty if I hadn't been."

***

Mark turned over yet again, keeping his knees bent, as he tried in vain to make himself comfortable. The sofa was too short to serve as a bed and his mind was too full of thoughts that refused to settle. What was he going to do about Esty in the morning? He couldn't really make plans because he didn't know how she would be. If she woke up in the same crazy state she was in when he found her, he supposed she would need some sort of medical treatment. If not, then it would depend on her. Presumably she would go back to where she was staying,

70

with whatshername... Noa.

What had happened to Esty? What could possibly have caused this? Why did she keep screaming, "Let me go. I'm bad."?

And why had no one contacted him? Surely if they were worried about where she was, they'd have asked him if he knew. Unless....

Mark leapt to his feet and snatched his phone from his bag. There was the message: "Mark. Esty is MISSING. If you know where she is please call me ASAP. Noa" The message followed three missed calls, all from the same number.

Of course. He'd put the phone in the bag as always, because it was uncomfortable to dance with it in his pocket. And he hadn't heard it ringing over the loud music. And he hadn't thought to look at it when he left the hall.

He looked at the time. 3:24. Would Noa be sleeping or would she be awake, still desperately trying to find Esty? Should he contact her now or wait till the morning? Would she be annoyed to be woken up or pleased to hear his news? How would he feel if the roles were reversed? He sent her a text message.

***

"Sorry about the mess," Mark said through the open kitchen doorway.

"Don't worry about it," said Noa. "I know what it's like when a lot of young people live together in a confined space."

Mark filled the kettle and turned it on. "How did it happen?" He'd told Noa the part he knew.

"I don't know. I went to collect Esty after the meeting at eight o'clock, as we'd arranged. She wasn't outside. I waited in the car for twenty minutes. I thought she must still be inside talking to her parents. When I went to ask the family who own the place, they told me they'd all left. In fact, Esty's parents had only been there for about ten minutes. Esty stayed a lot longer and then left. I've been going crazy with worry. I even called the police, but they said they couldn't do anything until she had been missing for 24 hours."

"I'm so sorry. I should have thought of phoning you earlier, but it was such a shock finding her like that. I couldn't think straight."

"Don't worry. I understand. I'm just happy Esty's safe. I was imagining all sorts of things."

Mark dropped teabags into two mugs and poured boiling water into them. He added milk to one and carried both to the table.

"Still British, I see," said Noa.

Mark shrugged. "I think I'll always take milk with my tea. I like it that way."

They sat opposite each other, silently sipping, both lost in their own thoughts at first.

"What on earth could they have said to her?" said Noa, continuing a thought.

"Perhaps it wasn't them. Something else could have happened. Someone could have said or done something to her after she left the house, before you arrived."

"It was them… or rather, him. My father. He made me realise what I've done."

Mark and Noa both turned towards the source of the quiet voice and exclaimed in unison. "Esty!"

She stood there, alone and fragile. Bare feet peeped out from beneath the long skirt. The long-sleeved blouse had been slung over the skirt, both equally crumpled. Her hair was in a mess, her eyes red.

Noa rushed to her.

Mark stood up, too. "I'll make some more tea."

"I'm so sorry. I've made you go without sleep."

"Not at all." Noa guided Esty to a chair at the table. "Have a seat. Mark's bringing tea. When you're ready, if you want, you can tell us what happened to you yesterday."

***

"So that's it." Esty clutched her mug in both hands, although its contents had long gone. "I don't know what happened to me last night. I guess I felt it was all too much. But I've thought about it now and I know I must go on with what I started. Despite this awful burden. I didn't think what I was doing and now I'll have to pay the penalty for the rest of my life."

Noa spoke softly. "If you'd known what was going to happen, would you not have left the community?"

"Of course not. Look how many lives I've ruined."

"But that's...." Mark struggled to make sense of Esty's position. "This is hard for me to understand. I was born into a society that has freedom of choice. I know what my parents would like me to do and what they wouldn't. But ultimately we all know that it's up to me to decide what to do with my life. I can't imagine a life with no choice."

"That's what extremism is all about," said Noa.

Mark turned to Esty. "It's not your fault that you were born into that family. You can't carry that burden all your life. That's wrong."

Esty shook her head. "That's what I have to do."

Chapter Twelve

For the rest of Friday and Saturday, Esty functioned as usual. She helped in the kitchen. She interacted with the children, talking and playing. She ate, but not much. Still, Noa eyed her with concern. Esty tried to stop her friend from worrying: "I'm all right, and besides, I'm not your responsibility," but she couldn't seem to find a way to convince her.

Mark phoned, asking after her and asking to speak to her. Esty declined. She didn't want to add to the pressure by having to sound happy to him. "Tell him it's not his fault. Tell him I'll talk to him in a day or two, when I feel up to it."

Noa continued to fret. "I'll phone Avi tomorrow," she said on Saturday. "He has more experience of these things."

"No, please don't do that. I'm all right."

"Esty, I have a responsibility towards you. When I see you in trouble, I have to do something. It would be wrong of me to ignore it. If I felt I could help you by myself, then I would. But this is something I have no experience of, so I need to inform someone who has. Avi."

Esty wasn't sure she wanted or needed to reap the benefits of Avi's experience. She worried that Avi might send her to therapy, the secular equivalent of consulting the rabbi. How could a therapist help? No one could change the facts. She had done something terrible and she would have to live with it for the rest of her life.

At about 9:30 on Saturday evening, Esty was in her room attempting to read a book on recent history when the doorbell rang. A few minutes later, she heard a knock on her door.

"Come in."

Noa opened the door. "Someone has come to see you. Can I

74

show her in?"

Esty raised her eyebrows. "Yes."

Another figure entered and Noa retreated, closing the door without a sound. Although the newcomer wore dark glasses and the head was covered with a scarf instead of her usual wig, Esty recognised the woman who stood still by the door.

"Mum!"

Rivka removed the glasses but kept the scarf on and remained by the door. "I came to tell you I'm proud of you."

"What!" Esty must have misheard. Proud?

"I think what you did was very brave. I couldn't tell you that when Dad was there, so I sneaked out this evening. He thinks I'm at the women's study evening. I didn't exactly tell him I was going there – I just let him assume."

"But… wait, have a seat."

"No, first I want to hug my lovely daughter who I haven't seen for so long, except for ten minutes while my hands were tied."

Mother and daughter stepped towards each other and fell into a warm embrace.

"Esty, I love you and always will, no matter what you do. You do know that, don't you?"

"I have to admit I forgot that for a bit, after our meeting on Thursday."

They sat side by side on the bed leaning against the wall, their legs stretched out in front of them. With her arm touching her mother's, their bodies so close together, Esty felt protected, even though she knew it couldn't last long. Soon Rivka would have to return to the rest of the family.

"I don't understand, Mum. You left the secular life to become haredi. So why are you proud of me for turning to the world you left?"

Rivka took a deep breath. "I was eighteen when I came to Israel. I wandered around the country, half of me taking in the amazing countryside and the ancient history while the other half was in a dream. I felt as if I was searching for something, but I didn't know what it was. Then somehow I got caught up in a women's seminary in Jerusalem, where they persuaded me that religion was the only way to go. We didn't keep any of the religion at home, so it was all new and fascinating for me. I threw myself into it and became more and more fanatical. My parents were devastated. They saw their only child separating herself from them. I didn't see it or I didn't care – I'm not sure which. I was positive that what I was doing was the only way to go."

"Why?"

"Because at the seminary they knew how to persuade us. They took young girls who were lost and gave them a reason for living. I was convinced that every haredi was good and pure, and I only had to follow them to live a perfect, happy life."

"Don't you think that any more?"

"The process of disillusionment was very gradual. It took me years to understand that for a haredi it's not about the relationship with God. It's about being seen to be good by other people. You do the right things not because you want to, or because you think that it's what God wants of you. That's how you explain it: 'God wants.' But really you do them so that people like Mrs Greenspan don't have anything to gossip about."

Esty stared open-mouthed, hardly believing these words were coming from the lips of her own mother. She had always thought of her as devout and God-fearing, sure of her convictions and her way of life. How could Esty have been physically close to her all these years without having any inkling of the doubts growing inside her?

Did Esty even agree with those words? She had grown up in that society. She had got to know many good, kind people. "It's true, there is a lot of that sort of thing," she told her mother. "But plenty of people really believe they're doing the right thing. They believe they're doing what God wants."

Rivka nodded at the rebuke from her daughter. "You're right. I think what I really mean is that I have reached the stage where I perform the actions just to please other people. In fact I reached that stage a long time ago."

"When you realised that was how you felt, why didn't you leave?"

"Because by that time I had a husband and a couple of children. And I wasn't as brave as you."

"You've never told me how you felt."

"I had to hide it all. I had to pretend to be a good wife and mother and ignore my inner thoughts. I certainly didn't want to make things hard for my children by causing them to doubt our whole way of life." Esty felt her mother's eyes on her, as if she'd only just noticed the trousers. "It seems I didn't succeed."

Again they embraced each other and stayed there, locked together for a minute or two until Esty pulled away to talk.

"Mum, you mustn't blame yourself. You were in a very difficult situation."

"I should have left when I knew I didn't believe in it any more."

"But you had obligations. It was much easier for me to do it. And you're brave, too. You've shown how brave you are by coming here today."

"I had to tell you how I felt. I didn't want you to think I disapproved like Dad."

"I'm very glad you came. I was so upset by what Dad said. I thought I'd made a big mistake."

Rivka shook her head slowly. "I'm the one who made the big mistake."

***

Long after Rivka had to leave to return home, Esty remained sitting on the bed pondering her mother's words. Rivka had explained that when they realised Esty was missing, they'd called in friends who could help to find her, and that was why she couldn't talk to Esty the first time she phoned. Even though these people were friends, it wasn't appropriate for them to discover the truth before Esty's father. She'd also mentioned Esty's second call, adding that she'd tried to get to the phone when it rang, but her husband had reached it first.

Esty had never understood before how Rivka felt. She'd never imagined her mother could be anything but happy with what she had. It was incredibly sad. A whole life changed by a decision made at age eighteen – a decision she'd later bitterly regretted. Esty herself was only nineteen. What made her think she was any better equipped to make a life-changing decision? Would her life pan out as she hoped? Would she be happy? Or would she end up like her mother, regretting her decision for ever after?

After some time, there was another knock at the door and Noa came in.

"I just wanted to make sure you're all right," she said.

Esty smiled at Noa's thoughtfulness, coming to check up on her but not coming too soon, before she'd had time to mull over this new development. "Yes, thank you. In fact I'm more all right than I was before."

Noa sat down on the edge of the bed. "Did your mother put your mind at rest, then?"

"She did more than that." Esty explained briefly what her mother had said.

"That's very sad for your mother, but wonderful for you that she's on your side."

Esty nodded. "Life is such a gamble. One wrong move and you can ruin it forever."

Noa looked straight into Esty's eyes. "Look at it the other way. One right move and you will always be thankful."

Chapter Thirteen

Esty was alone in the flat on Monday morning when the phone rang. As always, she had to force herself to answer it, quelling her fears that someone from the other world was going to force her to go back.

The caller came from this world, but Esty didn't want to talk to him either.

"How's it going?" Avi asked.

Esty put on a happy voice. "Fine. I'm studying hard. And Noa and her family have been wonderful."

"And?"

"And what?"

"Esty, it hasn't all been wonderful, has it? I've heard from Noa that there have been difficulties. I'd have been surprised if there hadn't been. You have undertaken something that's very difficult. No one sails through it. That's why we have meetings. So that you can talk to others who are going through similar difficulties. You are coming this evening, aren't you?"

"I'm not sure. I'm managing all right. I don't think I need to discuss this with anyone."

"Esty, I want you to try one meeting. You've got nothing to lose and probably plenty to gain. Even if you don't see any benefit in it, I think you owe it to all the people who have helped you to try it out."

"Okay." When he put it like that, it seemed she didn't have much choice.

"Can I have an assurance from you that you'll come to the meeting this evening?"

Now, Esty had no choice at all and she knew it. "Yes, I'll go."

An hour later, Esty took the bus to the Mahane Yehuda

Market off Jaffa Road – the *shuk*, as everyone called it. She'd volunteered to make the evening meal, a vegetable pie that had been a favourite in her home, and needed to buy the vegetables. She could have bought them in a local shop, but the shuk always had the best produce. And besides, Esty had always loved the shuk with its special noises and smells. She loved the way the vendors called out their wares. She delighted in the mingling aromas of herbs, coffee, melons, bread.

Of course, in such a place she was more likely to bump into her past. But she couldn't keep running away. She'd have to learn to face these people. Surely they'd prefer not to know her, anyway. They were probably more afraid of meeting her than she was of meeting them.

Esty walked along the alleyways, noting the quality and prices of the items she wanted. Potatoes, courgettes, carrots, onions. She revelled in the familiar sights, sounds and smells. With so much that was new and different for her, it felt good to return to this whiff of home.

"Sweet mangos. Only six shekels."

The loud voice just next to her startled Esty. How did these people keep shouting all day without getting sore throats?

Retracing her steps, Esty stopped at a stall selling carrots. "Could I have a bag, please?" she said to the vendor, a youngish man with black curly hair and a swarthy skin.

"For you, I'll give anything." The vendor's accent showed his Eastern heritage. Iraq or Syria or somewhere like that. The man himself was probably born in Israel, but he'd inherited the accent, the guttural As and Hs in particular. He reached up to a metal hook, tore off a plastic bag from the many hanging there and handed it to Esty.

Esty smiled, confident that his words weren't intended to lead anywhere, and picked out her carrots from the huge pile.

When Esty turned round after putting her last purchase into the shopping bag she'd taken from the flat, she spotted Mrs Greenspan and the same woman she'd seen in the shopping centre. At the same moment, the woman pointed towards Esty and the two began to stride purposefully towards her.

Esty panicked. She had to get away from these women, but how? She couldn't reach the bus stop, because the women were blocking that route. She could slip through the alley opposite her and double back along the parallel road, but that was wide and they'd spot her easily because it would be less crowded. So Esty stayed in the alleyway and started running away from the women, towards Jaffa Road. It was hard with the heavy bag, squeezing between the shoppers.

"Sorry," she called to a startled woman brushed on the leg by Esty's bag.

Glancing back, Esty saw the two women looking fierce and coming nearer. She turned and ran to Jaffa Road as fast as the heavy bag would let her. Now what? A train had just drawn up into the station. If she ran, she might just make it. With all her strength, she carried the bag over the railway lines and then across the little road. A car hooted but she ignored it. She had to get to that train.

Yes. The door opened to her touch and Esty entered, breathing heavily.

"There are lots of trains," said a stout woman sitting on a seat, her shopping bags at her feet. "You could have waited for the next one."

Esty didn't answer. She was still breathing too heavily. Besides, what could she say to the woman? I'm running away from two women who want to... what? What did they want to do to her? What could they do? She hadn't broken any civil law.

There they were. Those two evil women glaring at her through the window, desperately pressing the button in an attempt to open the door.

"Look at those two," said the stout woman. "You'd think their lives depended on getting on this train."

Not *their* lives, thought Esty. But it could be *her* life that depended on them not getting on.

The train glided off. Esty clutched a pole, taking deep breaths to regain her composure. When would she be safe from these people? Would she ever be safe from them?

***

When Esty entered the kindergarten that had been taken over for this evening's meeting, she saw several young people standing around chatting. They looked like any group of young people anywhere, or did they? The mostly dark clothes gave the impression of people trying to blend in rather than stick out. A man in the corner had a hand to his chin, as if stroking an imaginary beard. Another was swaying backwards and forwards in a motion he must until recently have used while praying.

As Esty surveyed the scene, she spied a girl she'd last seen before she'd taken the leap. The one who, under duress, had given Esty Avi's phone number. Would she be pleased to see Esty, or would she feel guilty about having helped someone else to escape?

The girl came over. "Esty – right? I'm Adi, now. Avigayil doesn't exactly trip off the tongue in these parts."

Esty smiled. "I was afraid you wouldn't want to know me, after I made you give me that phone number."

"I didn't want to be responsible for anyone else leaving. But if you left of your own free will, then I'm happy to see you here."

"I was so grateful for that number. It made it much easier for me, knowing I had a contact on the outside. How has it been for you?"

"Not easy, but I think the tide's beginning to turn. I feel as if I know where I'm going, even if it'll take forever to get there."

"What happened?"

Adi sighed. "It's a long story. Basically, I didn't realise when I left how long it would take. I want to learn graphic design, but first I have to pass the matriculation exams and I can only start doing that if I get a grant. In the meantime, I'm doing odd jobs like teaching bible studies privately to bored kids who need to pass the exam. What else could I do? It's all I know."

"That's hard," said Esty.

Adi nodded. "On top of that, I'm completely alone. My family has cut me off and they refuse to see me. I heard they mourned for me. Can you imagine it? Seven days of sitting at home and people coming to visit and offer condolences because, as far as they're concerned, I'm dead. Do you know what that feels like? Sometimes I wonder if I *am* dead – a dead person standing. It hurts so much to feel anything that I try to cut my feelings off."

Adi wiped a tear away with her finger. "I'm sorry. You must be going through a lot, too."

Esty shook her head. "Not as much as you." She didn't mention that she'd been one of those to offer condolences to the "mourning" parents, brothers and sisters. She'd gone because it had been expected of her, but she hadn't felt comfortable with the whole exercise.

The people were beginning to form a circle. Esty squeezed her body into a little chair. Some of the others preferred to sit on the floor. Esty noticed two who looked middle-aged. She thought how much harder it must be at that age, leaving everything you've known and starting afresh.

Avi welcomed Esty and one of the men to the group. Then he went round the circle, encouraging the members to bring up any issues they had. A middle-aged woman cried when she told the group that she wasn't being allowed to see her eight children for fear that she would "corrupt" them. "I know that in the end they'll have to let me see them," she said. "But in the meantime, I miss them so much."

Suddenly it was Esty's turn. She couldn't tell the group about meeting her parents; that was too private. Her father's frightening anger and what it had done to her were too embarrassing to reveal. Her mother's revelation definitely wasn't for their ears. Some of them were in contact with their families in her community. If the word got around of the non-believer in their midst, that would be devastating for Rivka and the whole family. In a way, it was fortunate that Esty had a newer event to share.

"I'm being followed. I escaped from them today, but what will happen if they catch me?"

"That's a common problem," said Avi. "Who else has been followed?"

A few raised their hands.

"There's nothing we can do about that. We can't protect you. If they take you somewhere, you have to be strong. You've escaped once and you can do it again, if you want to. If you escape again, they'll probably leave you alone after that, so it's really up to you. If you feel relieved to be back, knowing all the hardships outside the community, you can stay there."

Esty returned to her temporary home in a dream. She'd been very lucky. Some of those people were suffering a lot more than she was. She hoped Mrs Greenspan would leave her alone now. What if she didn't? What if she kidnapped her? Would Esty be strong enough to escape again? Or would she take Avi's other suggestion and stay in the world she knew with the people she loved – her brothers and sisters and mother and… yes, even her father. She didn't think she'd be happy doing that. She'd feel like a failure. And she'd miss people on this side. Noa had become a sort of substitute mother for her, helping her to work through the issues and giving her sound advice. And Mark – how could she live without him?

***

Esty didn't know what made her go out the next morning. Alone in the flat, she'd been swotting – studying local geography and history while listening to children's songs. Suddenly she had an urge to go out for a walk.

Beside the entrance to the building was the family's post box. Esty checked it, ready to go back to leave any letters in the flat. Putting her hand inside, she felt one solitary letter. She pulled it out of the box, feeling the extra-thick texture of the envelope. Examining it, she let out a gasp. It was addressed to her, in English. The top left-hand corner confirmed that it came from her grandparents.

In some trepidation, Esty took the letter to the nearby park. She imagined the worst-case scenario and started to dread this was what she'd find when she tore open the envelope: "Please don't write to us again. We lost our daughter twenty years ago and you have upset us very much by writing to us now."

***

Esty sat at the small, square table as the usual crowds thronged around her. Teenagers laughing together, their tee shirts sporting bizarre combinations of English words that made no sense. Young parents trying to keep their children in tow. People of all persuasions. At that thought, Esty lowered her head, letting her hair fall over her face. Would she ever be able to stop hiding?

Raising her eyes tentatively, she watched Mark as he carried the tray towards her, careful to avoid some very active children. He'd been so thoughtful and caring. He'd phoned her at Noa's and Gabi's place after she'd returned from her walk, worried that she hadn't answered his previous calls. "You should get a mobile phone," he'd said. This evening he'd collected her and taken her to the nearby Malcha shopping centre for coffee and cake.

Esty helped to lay out the drinks and cakes on the table. The cakes Mark had chosen each had two small round biscuits sandwiched together. "What are these?"

"Alfajores. They hail from Argentina. The filling is *dulce de leche*."

"Sounds good," said Esty, not really understanding much.

Mark returned the tray before sitting down. "So, will you finally tell me your good news?"

Esty couldn't stop herself from smiling. "I'm sorry – I should have told you before, but I wanted to keep it for this special occasion. I had a letter from my grandparents in London. They want to know me. They really want to know me. They wrote, "We're delighted to hear from you.""

"That's wonderful, Esty!"

"Not only that. They sent me some money with the letter and they said they want to pay for me to study. I didn't ask them to do that; they just offered. Isn't that fantastic? I'm going to see if I can start straight away. The only trouble is…."

"What?"

Esty took a bite of her alfajores. "Mmm. This tastes wonderful."

Mark beamed his pleasure. "I told you they're good. So what's the problem with your grandparents?"

"Well, they want to meet me and I want to meet them, but they don't fly any more because it stresses my grandmother too much and I can't go there because I'll be working and studying."

"You'll have holidays. You could go for the Sukkoth holiday. I'm planning to go then. I haven't seen my parents since I came here. Do you have a passport?"

Esty shook her head. "I've moved to a different world, but I've never visited another country."

Mark smiled. "You'd better get one soon. It's a good thing you're over eighteen, or your parents would have to sign for it. Whereabouts in London do your grandparents live?"

"In a place called Hampstead."

"Really? My parents are in Hendon. That's quite close. I was wondering, maybe…." Mark hesitated, apparently unsure whether Esty would approve.

"We could go together? Mark, I'd love that."

***

Too excited to fall asleep, Esty lay in bed reflecting on recent events. Her mother's visit, her grandparents' letter and this wonderful evening with Mark. Things were working out much better than she'd ever thought possible.

On the walk home this evening, side by side with Mark, he'd accidentally touched her hand and instantly apologised.

"No, it's all right."

Their hands touched again, this time on purpose, and remained linked. Esty felt something warm flow through her, as if the touch of his large, masculine hand completed an electric circuit. It felt daring but somehow right.

Now, as darkness slowed the currents in her mind, Esty reflected on the good things that had happened to her. She had the blessing of her mother, the prospect of a future good relationship with her grandparents and, above all, she had a good, kind man in her life.

Yet, despite all these good things, she couldn't dismiss the anger her father had shown towards her. If she hadn't left, he would have continued to be the loving parent he'd always been. And there was no doubt he was right. She had caused trouble for her whole family and she had no right to do that.

Whatever good things happened to her, now or in the future, would always be tempered by the bad things she had done by being selfish and stupid. Sometimes she was able to put such thoughts aside, but they never left her for long.

Chapter Fourteen

Esty watched as Shirli got into bed under the sheet. The little girl seemed quieter than usual.

"Which story shall I read you?"

"Nothing. I don't want a story."

"So let's sing a song."

Shirli wrinkled her nose.

Esty sat down on the edge of the bed, eying the little girl. "What's up?"

"Nothing's up."

"Did something happen in school?"

"No – only that my teacher is the annoyingest teacher ever. Ever and ever."

"What happened?"

"Lihi said I drew the picture on the wall but I knew it was her and Maya said I couldn't be the butterfly in the dance after she picked me and it's not fair cos it wasn't me who did it."

"Whoa – slow down. Who's Lihi?"

"She's a girl in my class. Not one of my friends."

"Who's Maya?"

"My teacher. I hate her."

"So Lihi drew a picture on the wall? Why did she do that?"

"She said it would look nice for the end-of-year party. I said we're not allowed to write on the wall but she said it's all right because it's the end of the year and the rules don't matter any more."

"Did anyone else see her draw it?"

"No. It was in the morning, before the others came."

"What happened when Maya saw the picture?"

"She was very angry. I thought if she knew who did it, it

would be bad for Lihi."

"Did she ask who did it?"

"Yes."

"What did you say?"

"Nothing. Lihi was already angry with me over the sweets. I didn't want to tell on her and make it worse."

"What sweets?"

"Yesterday I had some mint sweets and Lihi wanted one. I said I only had enough to give my friends and she's not my friend."

"So Lihi was angry with you?"

"Yes. She hit me on my arm and I did as if she wasn't there, and that made her angrier."

"And that's why you didn't say anything about the picture."

"Right."

"Then what happened?"

"Then Lihi said I drew it."

"Ooh, that's not nice."

"She's not a nice girl. That's why she's not my friend. When she said that, I said, 'I didn't draw it – Lihi did.'"

"What did Maya say?"

"She said Lihi must be right because she said it right away and I only said it after she said it was me. It's not fair."

"Oh dear. Tell me about the dance."

"It's called the Butterfly Dance and Maya chose me to be the butterfly because I'm the best one at dancing. Then when she thought I drew on the wall, she chose Netta to be the butterfly."

Esty patted Shirli's arm through the sheet. "You're right – it's not fair. Maybe your mummy can talk to Maya and tell her what really happened."

"She can't. It's too late – the party's tomorrow. Anyway, Maya will never believe me. She's very, very sure she's right. And I know she's wrong."

Esty gave Shirli a squeeze. "That's hard. But I'm sure you'll have many more chances to perform."

"Esty, why do grown-ups always think they're right?"

"Do they?"

"Yes. You can see they do from the way they talk."

"Perhaps they're not really as sure as they seem. Perhaps they pretend to be sure because they have to show they're in charge."

Shirli was quiet for a while. "Do you pretend like that?"

"Well, I'm certainly not always sure I'm right, but when I'm teaching in the kindergarten I have to show I'm in charge, so I suppose I do pretend sometimes. You see, teachers are only human beings. They don't know everything."

"What about when you're not being a teacher? Do you ever make mistakes?"

Esty thought about her recent past. About the way she left her family without thinking of all the repercussions. About the guilt she would always feel for the trouble she'd caused them. "Oh yes, I make mistakes."

"Did you have a teacher like Maya in the place you came from?" Shirli seemed to have readily accepted that idea of different worlds. She spoke as though she thought of them as two physically different worlds. Perhaps that was an accurate description.

Esty thought about her teachers – all women, of course. They had all sounded very sure of themselves, especially when it came to telling the girls about secular people and how bad they were. But she couldn't blame them for doing that. That's what they'd been taught to believe. They were shocked when Esty tried to question their statements. Hanna, for instance, when she'd talked about the utter selfishness of secular society.

"Surely they can't all be selfish," Esty had said in front of the whole class. "Don't they have soldiers who are willing to give up their lives for the rest of the people?"

"Esty!" Hanna had exclaimed. "How can you say such a thing? If they were good, pious people, they wouldn't need an army. The Holy One, blessed be he, would protect them as he does us."

90

Esty didn't reply. She certainly didn't want to let on that she'd secretly read a secular newspaper she'd found discarded in the street, and had learnt a lot from looking at a row of young, smiling men peering out of photos and a list of the locations and times of their funerals. After that incident in class, she kept her views to herself.

Did Esty's teachers ever wrongly accuse someone? They must have done. "I think I probably did have teachers like Maya," she replied to Shirli. "Maya shouldn't have jumped to that conclusion so quickly, but all teachers make mistakes, and sometimes the only thing you can do is to accept that life isn't always fair."

***

"Would you like to watch a programme with us?" Noa called out to Esty as she left Shirli's room.

Esty went into the living room to see Gadi sitting on an armchair and Noa on the sofa. The television was on, its sound muted. "Well, I really ought to do some more studying, but I am feeling a bit tired…."

"It's a new series. And it had a good write-up. It's time you watched some grown-up television."

Esty smiled. "All right. When you put it like that, it sounds as if it'll be good for my education."

"I think it will. Television is part of life on this side of the fence."

Esty joined Noa on the sofa. Gadi said, "Let's have a drink," and went to open the cabinet.

"I don't know…" Esty began.

"Aren't you used to drinking?"

"Only wine on the Sabbath and festivals."

"So have a little brandy with orange. That won't be any stronger than a whole glass of wine."

"I'll bring some nibbles," said Noa, standing up. She went off to the kitchen and returned a minute later with Bamba, Bissli and nuts. Even Esty recognised the peanut snack and the other flavoured snacks that were always prominent at all the children's parties she'd been to. In the meantime, a full glass of an orange drink had appeared on the low, oval table. Esty took a tentative sip. Then she took another with more relish. What a lovely taste. She helped herself to some nibbles and munched them, taking another sip of the drink in between. They went well together.

As the signature tune for the series began and the credits rolled up the screen, Esty put the glass on the table and sat back with a few peanuts in her hand.

The scene was a boarding school. The language used by the pupils was shocking. Most of their swearing consisted of words Esty hadn't even heard, or at least not in that context. Noa was right – this was quite an eye-opener.

And yet, these weren't bad kids. Several girls were comforting another girl whose parents had just split up. They seemed to really care for each other. Esty munched the peanuts as she watched.

Then the scene changed as it followed their teacher home to his wife. No, she couldn't be his wife because she was inviting him in, but... wow, she wasn't wearing much... he got to her breasts in a second and she was letting him do it ... enjoying his touch on her private parts, it seemed. Could Esty ever relax enough to enjoy something like that?

The scene changed again. It was dark and hard to make out... it seemed to be a bed and someone lying on his tummy under a blanket, going up and down... exercises?

"What's he d...?"

Esty stared at the screen, hardly believing what she was seeing. The man had rolled over. It was the teacher. Next to him lay the woman – the one he wasn't married to. He must have been on top of her, and when he was going up and down, he must have been....

Esty covered her face with her hands. In the background, she heard him telling the woman about things that had been happening at the school, but Esty was no longer interested.

"Are you all right?" Noa asked gently.

"No!" Esty ran to throw up in the toilet bowl.

When she'd finished, she washed her hands and face thoroughly and checked her face in the mirror. It was rather pale, but presentable. Then, with Esty's consent, Noa entered the bathroom and Esty saw her concerned face behind her own. It relaxed when Esty smiled.

"Fancy a cup of tea?"

***

"I'm sorry," said Noa, sitting down at the kitchen table. "I shouldn't have suggested that programme. I didn't know what was going to be in it, or how you would react to it."

"No, it's all right." Esty sipped her tea slowly. "I have to know about everything – the good and the bad."

"Do you think that was bad?"

Had Noa really asked this? How could there be any question? "Of course! They showed sex on television. That's something that should be private – between the man and the woman doing it. No one else should ever see it. And on top of that, those two weren't even married!"

Noa closed her eyes for a moment, then opened them and gazed at Esty as if from a distance away. When she spoke, her voice was soft and gentle, yet firm.

"You know they were only acting, don't you?"

"Yes, but…."

"And really the scene didn't show much. It was dark, they were under a blanket and we only saw a small movement apparently at the end of intercourse. The producer simply wanted us to know they'd had sex, but there was nothing specific."

"No…" Esty conceded. "But still, they weren't married."

Noa nodded, gradually opening her mouth to speak. "Welcome to the real world, Esty."

The sweet, warm tea soothed Esty, relieving the pain that had risen in her chest. "I didn't even think about that before I left… that in the secular world… people…"

"…indulge in sex before marriage?" Noa offered, her voice gentle, as if breaking some difficult piece of personal news to a young and innocent child. "Esty, it happens everywhere, all over the world. Even the community you came from isn't exempt from it."

"No, that can't be true. It goes against everything we're taught!"

"Sometimes people do go against what they've learnt, especially where animal instincts are concerned. They simply succumb to temptation and ignore their teachers. Probably some of those teachers are secretly breaking the rules they teach."

"I find that very hard to believe."

"It probably happens less in the haredi world. Most people obey the rules. But, on the other hand, those same rules can sometimes make sexual abuse more likely, not less."

Esty looked up from her mug, a frown creasing her forehead.

"I'm not saying it's common," Noa went on. "I think it's very rare. But there's a case featured in last weekend's newspaper and I think you should know. We're all only human beings. None of us is perfect. Some of us are better, some are worse. And it doesn't always matter where you've grown up and what you've been taught."

Noa's words echoed in Esty's head as she lay in bed that night. Could there be any truth in them? Could these things really happen in the moral, pious world in which she'd grown up?

Then she remembered Batya, a girl at school, only eight years old. Suddenly, she had disappeared. No one knew where she'd gone, although there was plenty of gossip. Rumours told of things she'd said. Lies she'd told about her own father.

At least, everyone had said they were lies….

Chapter Fifteen

A summer evening in Jerusalem. Such a pleasant time for a stroll, when the sun no longer burned down and a gentle breeze cooled your arms and face.

Esty was wearing a light, knee-length skirt with sandals and a top with sleeves that barely covered her shoulders. She'd taken to wearing lighter colours, now that she didn't feel so self-conscious in secular clothes. She felt liberated without the dark tights she'd previously always had to wear, whatever the weather. It was true what the people of her new world said. The norms of the haredi world originated in nineteenth century Eastern Europe. They simply weren't suitable for this country.

Mark looked good in his shorts, tee shirt and sandals. Esty slipped her hand into his, and smiled when he gave it a firm squeeze. She should really have been studying, but Mark had phoned to suggest a meeting and Esty was keen to see him again.

The sound of happy children came from the nearby play area. Mark and Esty continued along the path, hand in hand.

"Esty," Mark began, "what does *fillim* mean?"

"Fillim?"

"Yes. It's something to do with a camera. I heard someone say it, but I couldn't make out what they were talking about."

"Ah – it's what you had to put in the old cameras."

"You mean, film?"

"Yes, that's what they call it here."

Mark sighed. "It's like they take English and turn it into something else – Hebrish. Like something that happened at work today."

"What's that?"

"Someone mentioned that he'd gone to 'bough lin' yesterday evening. At least, that's what it sounded like. I thought he was saying something in Hebrew I didn't understand, but he said, no, it's English and he kept saying 'bough lin.' It was only when he wrote it down that I realised he meant 'bowling.' Apparently that's how they pronounce it here."

"Actually," said Esty, "I wouldn't know. It's not something I've ever talked about."

"What, you've never been bowling?"

"Does it look like the sort of thing haredi people do?"

"You know, it's hard to remember where you come from. You look so normal."

"Underneath, we're human beings – like everyone else."

"You're right. Actually, what's not allowed about bowling?"

"Nothing – I don't think it breaks any rules. It's simply not something we did."

"Why not?"

"Because it's a secular thing."

"So?"

"They didn't let us mix with secular kids."

"Why not?"

This was hard to explain. There were so many things, so many doctrines, that they'd taken for granted, never thinking to question them. Now Esty heard her teachers' words with new ears. "They said secular kids do bad things and we shouldn't see them."

"It sounds as if they were afraid you'd be influenced by them."

"I suppose they were."

Mark nodded. "Shows how confident they feel about their own way of life if they think they have to keep you away from any other way of life."

Esty didn't reply. Mark was right and he knew it.

"I must take you bowling. It's fun. What else haven't you done?

"I've never been to the beach."

"Really? But it's so close – only an hour's drive away."

"It wasn't thought suitable for me to see the way people behave at the beach – what they wear."

"Then I must take you to the beach, too. I wonder when we can go."

"How about Saturday?"

"Saturday." Mark drew the word out. "I usually go to synagogue on Saturday. I could skip it, or we could go after the service. If you can get transport into town to catch the taxi service – you remember there are no buses on Saturday."

Esty stopped walking. Her hand had somehow detached itself from Mark's. She stared at him, open-mouthed, horrified.

Mark stopped, too, and frowned back at her. "What's wrong?"

"You go to synagogue?"

"Yes." Mark sounded hesitant, bewildered.

"I didn't know. I thought you were secular."

"I thought you did know. That's how we first met. Well, not the first time, in the post office, but when we met properly."

"What do you mean?"

"Well, Sarah, the lady who invited us – she got to know me in the synagogue. And she knows I don't have any family here, so she's invited me over a few times."

Esty kept quiet, trying to absorb this new piece of information. It hadn't occurred to her before, although, now that Mark had explained, it fitted in. But it showed that Mark wasn't the person she'd thought he was. He didn't belong to the world she was attempting to be a part of. She'd thought she knew him, but now she knew she didn't.

"Esty, what's the matter?" Mark asked the question so softly that it took Esty time to take notice of it.

"Nothing, I… I have to… I think I'll go back now, if you don't mind."

"I'll walk back with you."

"No, I'll go on my own. I'll be all right."

***

As usual when he was upset or confused or worried, Mark began to walk.

Stupid. Why did he mention the synagogue? He should have kept quiet about it.

No! He didn't need to be embarrassed about it. So what if he attended synagogue? He always had, from before he could remember. It was part of who he was. And besides, how could he have known how Esty would react?

He should have known. He should have been more observant. Observant in the sense of seeing, of course, not in the sense of being orthodox. It should have been obvious how she felt.

But it wasn't. And even now, after what had happened, he couldn't answer the questions. Why? How? What now?

Somehow, as if there was only one way to go, as if this was the place to which all roads led, Mark found himself standing on the path that led to his block of flats, imagining a familiar voice behind him. At least, that's what he thought.

The tap on his shoulder was real. So was the voice, he realised.

"Hey, *mon ami*. Why you no hear me?" Then the voice's owner looked into Mark's face. "Something happen, right? Something bad. Come upstairs. You tell Papa Claude everything."

Mark wasn't sure that was what he wanted, but it seemed he didn't have a choice.

***

"But why she care you go to pray? It is not like you are one of them – *un pingouin*."

"A penguin?"

"Yes – all black with a little white in the front."

Despite everything, Mark couldn't help smiling at the description.

"Listen to Papa Claude. He know about *les femmes*. You have two choices. The one, you forget her – find a new girl. The other, you ask her why. If she say she want something and you want something else, you make – how you say – *un compromis*."

"A compromise," said Mark.

"Ah English, it is so like French. Not like Hebrew." Claude screwed up his face at the thought of the language he was attempting to learn.

"Hebrew isn't hard to learn, Claude. You just have to work at the vocabulary. And compromise is *pshara*." If Claude was superior to Mark in the fields of life and love, at least Mark had acquired more of the lingo.

"You see? Why *pshara*? Why they not use *compromis*?"

***

Left to his own thoughts at night, Mark recovered none of his previous optimism. Neither of Claude's options seemed at all possible. He couldn't ask her. Obviously that was out of the question. After the way she left him, he was sure she wouldn't even agree talk to him again. The alternative? To forget her? Impossible. He could never do that.

***

Esty was sure of herself. Of course she was. She had been determined to leave the haredi world and become secular and she had done precisely that. Every other decision would be easy compared to that one. If she ever became attached to a man, he would be secular, too. She'd had all she could take of religion. Religion, for her, was all about doing the right things to satisfy friends, neighbours, the community. No more. She'd left her home, her family and her life to be free of all that.

She'd been deceived by Mark. No, that sounded bad. He hadn't purposely deceived her but, albeit unintentionally, he'd led her to believe that he was secular, too, and therefore someone she could form some sort of romantic attachment with. It was a misunderstanding. Now that she knew he was orthodox – or maybe "traditional," she conceded – she knew he couldn't be the one for her. She was finished with him. Her life would now continue without him. There was no question. Esty was absolutely certain.

So why was she so miserable?

***

Esty went to the kitchen after reading Roey his bedtime story. She made herself some tea, intending to take it to her room and get on with some studying. As she was leaving with the mug, Noa came.

"Don't go. Let's have a drink together."

"All right. I'll make it for you."

"Thanks," said Noa.

Noa waited until Esty sat down opposite her before asking, "What happened?"

"What do you mean?"

"I know you're going through a difficult time. It isn't easy to make such big changes. But today you seemed particularly down. Something happened to make you very upset. Right?"

Esty sipped her tea before replying. "It's not something that happened. It's something I did."

Noa gazed at Esty, her eyebrows raised.

"I walked out on Mark."

Noa's mouth dropped open and her eyes gave a slow blink. "Why?"

"Because it turns out he's orthodox."

"Not orthodox exactly – only traditional."

"So you know."

"Yes, that's how he met Sarah. I thought you knew that."

"Everyone thought I knew. But I didn't."

"And now you do. Why does it matter?"

"Because I left religion to become secular. I don't want to have anything to do with religious people."

"Mark isn't religious. He's traditional."

"People keep coming out with this "traditional" word as if it's another sort of "secular," but I can see it isn't. It involves synagogues and rabbis and kosher food and God knows what else."

"Esty, you're entitled to your views. Everyone is. But I think you're judging something you don't know about. You should find out more before rejecting it."

"I don't…." Esty stopped. Actually there was some sense in what Noa said. It was wrong to judge practices she didn't know about, just as it was wrong of her teachers to judge all those who weren't haredi without really knowing anything about them. Or the other way round, for that matter. "How can I find out more?"

"Well, not from me, obviously, but I'm sure Mark could explain."

"Mark! I can't ask him after leaving him like that. I'm sure he won't want to talk to me again."

Chapter Sixteen

"Surprise! Guess who!"

"Claude! How did you know?"

"Know what?"

"That it's my birthday today." When Claude didn't answer immediately, Mark added, "You did know, didn't you?"

"But of course. Claude, he know everything."

Mark couldn't see. Blocking his vision was not Claude's hands but material. Thick, dark material that Claude was tying behind his head.

"Hey – cut it out. I guessed it was you."

"Ah, but I have more surprise. A birthday present."

"All right. Do I have to feel it and guess what it is?"

"Yes, but it is not here. We go in a car."

"What car? Whose car?"

"No questions. You come with me."

"But how can I know it's safe?"

"Mark! Now I hurt. You no trust your friend?"

Mark sighed and stood up, submitting to being guided out of the flat, down the stairs and into the back of a waiting car driven by someone who must have communicated with Claude in sign language.

A few minutes later, the car stopped and he was bundled out and into a building, he thought, and then into a room.

"You wait here with me," said Claude. "Your present will come."

"This is crazy. You're crazy."

"No, my friend. It is you who is crazy."

The door opened and closed. Mark sensed the presence of at least one more person in the room. Claude took his hand and joined it to another hand, smaller and smoother than his own. With his other hand, Mark reached over and felt long straight hair hanging down from a head lower than his. "Esty?"

"Yes."

"But…."

"Shh."

Mark felt his blind being removed. He blinked and opened his eyes in time to see Noa removing a blindfold from Esty's eyes.

"You see? You are crazy. All the two of you."

"He's right." Noa's eyes twinkled. "Each of you refused to talk to the other because you were sure the other one didn't want to talk to you. So Claude and I had to concoct this plan to bring you together. And now we're leaving you here to talk, so you'd better do it."

The door opened and closed again, and Mark and Esty were alone in the room.

"Mark, I'm so sorry. I should never have walked out on you like that. When I thought about it, I knew it was a mistake, but then I thought it was too late and you'd never want to talk to me again."

Mark shook his head. "I think they're right. We are both crazy. I was sure you'd never agree to talk to me again."

"Let's sit down. I want you to tell me what traditional means."

They sat side by side on the sofa.

"It means doing certain things because that's what our people have done for thousands of years. It means meeting like-minded people who want to do those things together and get together socially. It means not being extreme – neither one way nor the other."

"Why? Why is it important not to be extreme?"

"At one extreme, there are the 'holier-than-thou' people, who turn it into a competition. They say, 'Look at me. I'm denying myself more than you are, so I must be better than you.' It's as

104

if they're vying for God's favour, although really God doesn't come into it."

"You don't have to tell me about them."

"And also the ones who find all sorts of ways of getting round the laws they themselves created."

Esty nodded her agreement. "Like Sabbath lifts and the *eruv* – that piece of wire that turns the whole city into an enclosed area, enabling them to carry on the Sabbath. As if carrying a tissue outside is work, but connect a piece of wire and you can carry a whole parcel of books because that's not work."

"Exactly. At the other extreme, there are people who are lost, don't know where they're going or where they belong, have no purpose in life."

"But I've met secular people. They seem happy."

"Some of them cope with it, others don't."

"I'll cope with it."

"You're strong, and you know what the other extreme is like. But what about your children?"

"What about them?"

"Well, look at your family. Your grandparents are secular, right? And they seem happy that way. But your mother rebelled against it and went to the other extreme. Then you left all that. What do you think your children are going to do?"

"If I'm happy, why shouldn't they be happy the same way?"

"I don't know. Why wasn't your mother happy?"

Esty cast her mind back to what her mother had revealed during her surprise visit. "She was lost and she thought religion gave her a reason for living."

"If she'd known anything about religion beforehand, she wouldn't have gone there, right? She would have known enough not to let them persuade her. That's why I think extremism is bad, whether it's religious, political, or whatever. Compromise is the way to go in any relationship, including the one with God."

They were silent for a while. Esty had never heard Mark

being so forceful before. Perhaps that was because they hadn't had such a serious discussion until now. It showed her what he was like. Although he often seemed shy and quiet, it was clear he could show his mind when he wanted to. She liked that. And what he'd said made a lot of sense, especially about the back-and-forth pattern in her family. How would she feel if her children went the other way? Noa was right – Esty had been too quick to judge.

"Tell me about your synagogue," she said.

Chapter Seventeen

The offices of the Interior Ministry had always been located in Shlomtsiyon Hamalka Street, just behind the main post office. Other government offices had moved, over the years, into modern, impressive new buildings. But the Interior Ministry had remained in place. The only change had been when it took over some additional space in the building to add a second lift and some new rooms. Esty remembered being there with friends just three years before. They'd gone to receive their identity cards, chatting all the time, comparing their answers on the forms they had to fill in, and feeling very grown up to be getting their own identity cards. When they'd finished filling in the forms and before their numbers appeared on the screen, they'd also compared the photographs they were required to provide and their parents' identity cards, which they had to bring for identification.

Esty had brought her mother's identity card. She remembered her friend Leah having noticed under place of birth the words, "United Kingdom."

"Where's that?" she'd asked.

"It's the country that consists of England, Scotland, Wales and Northern Ireland," Esty had told her.

But Leah hadn't even heard of England. What wasn't in the bible wasn't part of their curriculum.

"Is the United Kingdom part of America?" Leah had asked.

"No, it's part of Europe. Have you heard of that?"

She had. But only because all her great grandparents had come from Europe in the 1930s – a time that, for Leah, might as well have been centuries ago.

This time, Esty was here on her own. But that was fine. She

was fully able to manage her own affairs now. She proceeded through the narrow entrance watched by a guard, then opened her bag and showed it to a second guard before walking through the metal detector. The two guards chatted together non-stop. The signs directed Esty to the second floor.

Several people stood waiting for the lifts, including two with prams. Esty decided to climb the old staircase.

The procedure was quite efficient. At one window, Esty received a form to fill in and a ticket with a number. She sat on one of the grey metal seats to fill in the form and had only just finished when her turn came.

The clerk read through the form, then looked back at Esty and frowned. "Are you sure that's where you live?"

"It's where my parents live. Where I live now is just temporary. When I move to somewhere more permanent, I'll change the address on my identity card."

The clerk nodded. "I see. I wish you luck."

Esty understood the remark. Just by seeing her parents' address and looking at the way she was dressed, the clerk knew that she'd recently gone over to the other side.

"Thank you."

Putting the receipt for her passport application in her bag, Esty made for the stairs to go back down to the entrance. She reached the exit from the office just as a mother was wheeling a pram from the other department on that floor – the one for registering births and deaths. Esty recognised her and, without thinking, called out, "Leah!"

Leah looked up and stood for a moment staring at Esty, her mouth wide open. Esty was also transfixed, but she took in the pram that held two children, one of them probably a new-born, whose birth had to be registered here. By Leah's side was another child, dressed as a boy but with long straight hair. Of course. Boys under three couldn't have their hair cut. It was odd how practices that had always seemed so normal were beginning to feel strange.

The boy started to call. "Mummy. Come." Suddenly, Leah turned away from Esty and continued to wheel the pram to the lift. She hadn't said a word.

Esty went down a few stairs and then sat on one of them. She had no wish to bump into Leah again on the ground floor. If anything brought out the difficulties of leaving the community, it was this meeting with an old friend. Even though Esty had always known this sort of behaviour by friends and acquaintances was likely, when it really did happen it came as a terrible shock.

Esty and Leah had grown up together. They'd played together, sung songs together and talked of their dreams for the future, the men they hoped they'd marry. True, they'd seen less of each other since Leah had got married, especially when her babies began to arrive. But when they'd met, Leah had always seemed pleased to talk to her childhood friend again, and delighted when Esty cooed over one of the babies.

Now, Leah wouldn't even say hello to Esty. Probably all her old friends would react in the same way. The incident brought home to Esty what it meant to cut yourself off from everything you'd ever known and begin again with nothing.

A man coming down the stairs stepped round Esty and then looked back at her. "Are you all right?"

"Yes, thank you." Esty heaved herself up and continued down, confident that Leah and her entourage would have left by then.

***

With time to spare before she had to go to meet Mark, Esty decided to wander around the town centre. She walked back up Jaffa Road and turned into the pedestrianised Ben Yehuda Street.

At one time, she'd heard, the three streets – Jaffa Road, Ben Yehuda Street and King George Street – had formed the only leisure place in West Jerusalem. Known as "the Triangle" it contained almost the only shops and restaurants as well as several cinemas. Now, the cinemas had all gone and Jerusalem had expanded, but still, this was the place for shops, restaurants and night clubs. Esty climbed the street slowly looking at the variety of shops – clothes, shoes, books, gifts and more.

One day, when she was settled and earning a proper living, she would treat herself to one of those tasty looking meals at the restaurant she passed, and sit out here in Ben Yehuda Street watching life going on all around her. Now, she contented herself with buying falafel and salad in pita from a bar and eating it standing up by a long, high, shelf-like table. Even that felt like luxury. Growing up, she never ate in a restaurant. There was never enough money. If she had, she knew that before buying any food she'd have had to examine the certificate closely to make sure the place was kosher enough for them. If the certificate came from an authorising board that wasn't good enough for them, or if the date on the certificate had lapsed, they couldn't eat there.

Today, Esty kept her eyes away from the certificate and felt happy and free, especially after her meal when she bumped into Koren, the kindergarten teacher she was going to work with. The friendly meeting put the previous one with Leah into perspective. Her old friends wouldn't talk to her, but she could make lots of new friends who would.

By the time she needed to start going to keep her appointment with Mark, Esty walked jauntily, almost skipping back along Jaffa Road. Life was going to be good. She would concentrate on the new people and events, and forget about the old ones.

Her route, this evening, would lead her past Yemin Moshe, where she had revealed her past to Mark, and on along Emek Refaim Street to Lloyd George Street. Mark had described the quaint cinema tucked in behind a bar frequented by young people. Esty was looking forward to seeing it.

She passed all sorts of people on her walk. Some were Arabs. You could tell them by the scarves some of the women wore – the sort that covered the base of the chin. Jewish women who covered their hair with scarves always tied them behind the neck. Some of the Arab women also wore their traditional dresses. None of them ever covered their faces, as she'd heard some did, even in Europe.

There were plenty of orthodox Jews around, many of them haredi. Not so long ago, Esty had felt part of them. Now they were beginning to feel like aliens, while those dressed in normal western clothes – even the girls in very revealing tops – had started to feel like the group closest to her. She could almost sense this process of change, like…. Yesterday, on the television, she'd seen a speeded up film of a little bud transforming into a big, beautiful red rose. That was the way she looked back at the change in her.

They must have been hiding in a shop entrance. Esty didn't notice them at all. Not until they each grasped one of her arms, turned her round and pulled her so strongly that she had no choice but to walk in that direction.

"Don't try anything silly," one of them said. Esty recognised the whiny voice. "You wouldn't want to cause your family any more trouble by creating a disturbance here on this secular street."

Of course she didn't. She hadn't ever wanted to cause them trouble. Now, finally, her punishment had come. She deserved whatever they were going to do to her.

"Who…" she began and stopped. If her father had requested this, she didn't want to find out from Mrs Greenspan.

"What did you say?" Mrs Greenspan's whiny voice had lost its false friendliness of previous meetings. Now it sounded as Esty had always thought it should. Evil, cunning, wicked.

"Where are you taking me?"

"You'll see soon enough."

She did. Despite the heat, Esty shivered on the familiar

doorstep, still held by these two strong women. A familiar doorbell rang in her ears.

Esty shivered again when she saw her mother's shocked face behind the open door.

The two women pushed Esty inside and then entered the flat themselves, closing the door behind them.

Another door opened before Mrs Greenspan said, "We found her in King George Street. Look at these secular clothes she's wearing. She's a disgrace to our community."

Esty's father strode to the door and opened it. "Thank you, Mrs Greenspan."

"But…" Mrs Greenspan began. "I understand. I'll come back later," and the two women left. Esty's father closed the door and returned to face her.

Esty stood still where they'd pushed her, her back to the front door, her hands clasped in front of her, as if that could hide her trousers from everyone. Suddenly finding herself back in this place where trousers were considered men's clothing and strictly forbidden for women, Esty was deeply ashamed. She kept her head down, afraid to face her father. What would he do to her now? The more time went past the more she was sure it would be something awful. But she deserved it, whatever it was.

Eventually he spoke. "I'm sorry, Esty."

Esty looked up, frowning.

"As much as I disapprove of what you have done, I would never try to bring you back by force. Those women did something wrong."

"So you didn't…."

"No, Esty. I didn't ask them to bring you, and I'm going to let you go. Rivka, please bring something to cover her face so that she's not recognised in our neighbourhood."

As Rivka rushed to their bedroom-cum-living-room, Esty, still with her back to the front door, somehow felt an extra presence in the little hall. She raised her head cautiously to spy some familiar little faces peeping out from each of the two rooms. Seeing them made her realise how much she'd been missing them all, and she longed to run to them and hug her sisters and ask them what they'd been doing. She wanted to apologise for the trouble she'd caused them, and try to explain why she'd done it.

Her father must have noticed the changed expression on Esty's face. He turned round. "Get back inside and close the doors. All of you." He sounded stern but controlled.

Then he turned back, and Esty saw and felt the window of hope closing as the faces vanished and the doors closed. "Couldn't I just say hello to them, now that I'm here?"

"I told you, Esty. No contact with your brothers and sisters. I can't allow you to confuse them further."

Tears welled up in Esty's eyes. She had known this would probably happen. When Avi had asked on the phone on that first day, she had said she was prepared to be cut off from her family. But now that it was happening, it was much worse than she'd ever imagined. The sight of those little faces had caused her heart to ache. How could her father be so cruel?

Then she remembered that she was the cruel one. She had created this situation by running away in the first place. She had caused her family to suffer. Her father was only reacting to her terrible deed.

Esty forced her mind back to what had just happened and the question that was nagging her. "What if she does it again?"

"Mrs Greenspan won't kidnap you again. She'll be expecting me to give her some compensation for her effort. But she won't get any."

Rivka returned with an old scarf that she tied round the front to cover most of Esty's face.

"Goodbye Esty." Her father opened the front door.

Esty longed to hug her mother, but sensed it would be inappropriate just now. She hoped Rivka would pay her another secret visit before too long.

"Goodbye. And thank you." Esty turned and hurried out,

keeping her head bent until she was back on Jaffa Road. Here she removed the scarf and stuffed it into her handbag. Then she ran all the way to Lloyd George Street, not stopping once.

***

Mark looked down the street. Still no sign of Esty. She really needed to get herself a mobile phone. No need for anxiety in this day and age. Perhaps he could buy her a phone. Or would that make her think he was hinting at something?

It wasn't like Esty to be so late. Mark glanced at his watch. The film was due to start now. He toyed with the tickets in his pocket. Of course he couldn't go into the cinema. He had to wait for her because he had the tickets. And besides, she wouldn't know where he was. What could have happened to her?

There. Yes, she was coming, running for all she was worth. No need for that. Mark waved. Then he caught sight of her face, and saw the tears streaming down.

"Esty…." She was sobbing. It pained him to see her like this. He wanted to hold her close to him, but was still afraid of doing something she wasn't yet ready for. When she buried her face in his shirt, he put his arms round her and stroked the back of her head.

Gradually the sobbing and shaking subsided and Esty's red eyes appeared. "Mark, I'm sorry. I can't watch the film, but you go."

"No, the film doesn't matter." Mark looked down at Esty. Even in this state, her beauty shone through. She needed help. That was clear. He wasn't sure that he was the person to provide it, but right now he was the only person available. "What happened?"

Esty looked around at the young people shouting, laughing. "Can we go somewhere else? Somewhere quiet?"

Mark tried to think. This bar wasn't suitable. They probably

114

wouldn't find a free table. And none of the nearby cafes and restaurants would be quiet at this time of the evening. Behind and quite close was a children's play area. That should be quiet now. "Come." Keeping one arm round Esty's waist, he guided her to the place.

***

"I should never have done what I did. I will have to suffer my punishment for the rest of my life."

They were sitting on the wooden bench in the corner. The swings swayed in the breeze, as if ridden by ghostly, silent children. Opposite them, the tall, thin houses looked distinctive. Not because of their facing made of Jerusalem stone – that was a common feature of the buildings in this city. No, it was the windows with their arched tops and, even more so, their steep roofs. Mark half-closed his eyes and the image of the house opposite merged with his impression of Mrs Greenspan – tall and thin with a witch's hat.

Esty's words had stung Mark. She was a good person. She didn't deserve to suffer at all. These people needed to leave her alone. He tried to reassure her: "But your father said it wouldn't happen again."

"So there'll be different punishments – I don't know what. Whatever they are, I deserve them all."

Mark laid a hand on Esty's thigh. He longed to reach over and embrace her. "No, Esty. You've done nothing wrong. Everyone has a right to choose for themselves. No one should have to suffer all their life simply because of a quirk of fate. And besides…." Mark gazed at Esty, willing her to understand, to come to terms, to get past this period of transition and self-doubt. Willing her to be happy and confident. "If you hadn't left your community, you and I would never have met, and I would have been deprived of a wonderful friend."

Esty shook her head. "That's very kind of you to say that,

115

but…"

"No, it's not kind. It's the truth. It's what I know. And it's what you must believe. Do you think the Mrs Greenspans of this world are the good people? No, they're nasty… evil. They only want to cause mischief. Forget about her. Forget about them all. You are where you need to be now. That's all you need to remember."

"But people are suffering because of what I did."

"I bet that's only temporary. Sooner or later, things will settle down and so will you – here, where you belong."

Esty shrugged her shoulders. "I hope so."

Chapter Eighteen

Esty sat on her towel contemplating her next hurdle. Above her, a large wooden roof, held up by four poles, protected her pale body from the sun. When would these hurdles be over? When would they subside and become normal events? Everyone around her was doing it. Why was she so scared?

The service she had attended that morning had been strange, especially the seating arrangement – men and women next to each other. Sitting next to Mark in a synagogue would take some getting used to. But no part of the service had been difficult because there was nothing she had to do. Also, once she'd got used to the initial weirdness, the service itself had been mostly the one she was familiar with. It was really quite a marvel that people who were so different recited the same words and performed the same actions, standing and sitting at the same parts of the service, reciting familiar blessings in turn, carrying the torah scroll in a procession around the synagogue.

The congregants had been very friendly and welcoming. By the time they left, Esty had begun to believe she could get used to this place and these people.

Then, as planned, they'd gone back to change at Mark's place before setting off for the beach. Esty had found it hard to reconcile the two things on the same day, but Mark's explanation had seemed logical.

"Today is the day of rest. There's nothing to say we aren't allowed to rest on the beach."

So here she was, hugging her legs on the towel, and all she had to do was to take off her skirt and tee shirt to reveal the new swimming costume underneath. Then she could join Mark in the water that looked so inviting. She looked around at the other people. The children licking ice creams. The youngsters and not-so-youngsters playing that popular game with bats and balls – *matkot*. Women of all sizes and shapes dressed only in swimming costumes or bikinis. No one would take any notice of Esty if she took her outer clothes off. She would simply look normal – like everyone else.

She looked out to sea. There he was, bobbing in the waves with lots of other people, looking back at her every so often. She'd said she'd join him, that she only needed time. He'd understood and left her to overcome this hurdle on her own, ready to congratulate her as soon as she jumped over it.

He looked wonderful in his swimming trunks – slim, strong, masculine. She'd been struck dumb at the sight. This man… her man… the man who could be hers if she could only….

In a second, she jumped up, threw off her skirt and tee shirt, and ran to the sea, to Mark, to his outstretched hand.

***

Mark loved the sea. He loved the relaxing feeling of floating on its surface, being tossed by the waves, submitting to their power. But today he was plagued with doubts. Was he right to take Esty to that service that was so alien to her? Could she cope with the ride to the beach immediately after that?

And what now? Could she overcome her fears and come to join him in the sea? Or would she remain there hunched up on the towel, cursing him for causing her embarrassment. He looked back again and there she was, running towards him in a swimming costume that hugged her slim, feminine body perfectly.

Mark swam towards her, to the shallower water. Then he stood and reached out his hand and she took it, letting him guide her in… well… unfamiliar waters.

"Well done," he said, and she smiled so sweetly that he wanted to hold her close to him and embrace her with his love.

He had to use all his power to restrain himself, still fearing that too much, too soon, would spoil everything forever.

Esty jumped as a wave climbed up her body and dispersed. "This is amazing. It all feels so new and exciting. I had no idea it was like this."

Mark gave her hand a squeeze. Was she only talking about the sea? Or did she mean the whole experience? Was he involved in these new and exciting things? Or was he simply her guide and mentor, introducing her to all the things she needed to learn about in her new life? When he had taught her all he could, when she had experienced enough of her new world to feel part of it, would she swim away and leave him gazing after her?

***

It felt very strange to be in water, almost naked, with so many people around, even though no one was looking at her. Except for Mark, of course. He was looking delighted. Was it just because she had managed to overcome her doubts, or was it because he liked to see her body. Perhaps, after all, she was being too brazen.

After a while, the excitement had gone, replaced by more doubts. Esty let go of Mark's hand, saying, "I think that's enough for now." Then she ran back to the wooden shelter and wrapped herself up in her towel. She sat down on the sand and drew her legs up, trying to cover as much of them as she could. She kept her head facing down. Surely she hadn't done anything very terrible. After all, everyone else was doing it. But to show herself off to Mark like that. How could it be right?

"You won't get dry like that."

Esty raised her head to see Mark towering over her, a sly grin on his face.

Mark spread his towel out in the sun and lay down on it. Despite everything, it gave Esty a thrill to see his body

119

glistening from the sun's rays.

"Won't you get burnt like that?"

"No, I don't think so. The sun isn't so strong now. Won't you join me? It'll be more comfortable to put your clothes on over a dry swimming costume."

There was sense in Mark's message. But Esty's courage had left her now. She shook her head. "I'll just have to be uncomfortable." It was warm here in Tel-Aviv, warmer than Jerusalem. Nothing would happen to her if her body was a bit damp.

They sat for a while, eating the sandwiches they'd brought and watching the sea and the people as they packed up and left the beach. Then Esty put her clothes back on and so did Mark.

"Are we leaving now?" Esty asked.

"You can't leave now without watching the sunset. It won't be long."

So they sat and talked, and before long the sun began to change colour as it dropped down to the horizon over the sea.

"How beautiful," said Esty.

"Wait, it gets better."

And it did, going a deeper and deeper red and lowering itself into the sea, a semicircle getting smaller, a dot that vanished.

"Wasn't that worth waiting for?"

"Oh yes."

They held hands and continued to sit for a while, side by side on their towels.

By the time they left the beach, the buses were starting up after the Sabbath. They took one to the bus station and caught another bus to Jerusalem.

As their bus swung round into the Jerusalem bus station, Esty said, "Mark, you don't have to come back with me. I can easily get back on my own from here."

But Mark wouldn't hear of it. "It's no problem. And I'll be happy to have a little more time with you."

Esty should have been pleased, but somehow she wasn't. She

felt as if she was being treated like a little girl who couldn't manage on her own, although she knew that wasn't true. Or maybe the ordeals of the day had been enough for her, despite the enjoyment, and she needed to be alone. She wasn't clear in her own mind what exactly was bothering her.

Perhaps it was neither of those. Perhaps she had a forewarning of what she was going to find when she got back to her temporary home, and knew that she didn't want Mark to be part of it.

Chapter Nineteen

There she was as Esty pushed the front door open. She stood facing Esty and Mark with Noa's mothering arm round her shoulders.

Esty stood for a moment in shock. Then she dropped her bag and rushed to hug the newcomer. "Gila! How lovely to see you. What are you doing here?"

Behind her, Esty heard Noa telling Mark in a soft undertone, "She's her sister."

Mark replied, "I can see that."

Esty and Gila had been taken for twins before, despite the almost three years between them. Their faces were very similar, and Gila had matured faster than Esty had. Gila was always the wild one of the family. Even as a young child, she'd always been obstinate, fighting to get her way.

Esty had admired her little sister and had always tried to stick up for her. Of all her siblings, Gila had been the closest. But now Esty was afraid for her sister. She stepped back from her frowning.

"Gila, did you get permission to come and see me?"

"Esty," Noa interrupted. "Why don't you go into the living room. Gila has something to tell you."

Noa was smiling, but Esty still worried. Something wasn't quite right.

Mark hesitated at the doorway. "I think I'd better leave you to it."

"No, don't go," Gila piped up. "I've hardly met you, but Noa has told me all about you and I'm sure, as you know so much about our family, it'll be all right for you to hear this, too. You too, Noa. You know it all, anyway."

Esty didn't feel so sure about this arrangement, but after Gila had invited Mark, Esty couldn't very well tell him to go. So she found herself sitting in the living room with Mark and Noa, and Gila who she really wanted to talk to on her own. She tried to ignore the other two and concentrate on her sister.

"Esty, I'm in trouble at home and I need your help."

Esty nodded. She had guessed as much. "So you didn't get permission to see me."

"No. Things have been hard since you left. Mum and Dad are worried in case any of us decide to follow you. And they're worried about me especially."

"Why you?" Esty decided not to mention that their mother was probably less worried than their father. That business needed to remain a secret between their mother and Esty. She glanced at the other two, hoping they wouldn't say anything, either.

"Because I'm old enough to make decisions for myself. And you know how obstinate I am. So they're desperately trying to marry me off now."

"But you're only sixteen!"

"That's old enough to marry. Mum and Dad think they made a mistake with you, letting you put off choosing a husband. And they don't want to make the same mistake with me."

"Why can't you tell them that you're not ready for marriage, but that you won't do what I've done so they don't need to worry?"

"Because that wouldn't be true."

"What do you mean? What wouldn't be true?"

"I want to leave the community, Esty. I want to be secular, like you."

"No! You can't."

"Yes I can. I've decided."

"You're only sixteen. How can you know that?"

"If I'm old enough to get married, I'm old enough to decide

to leave the community. Besides, if I stay any longer they'll make me get married and then it'll be harder to leave."

Esty had run out of things to say. What an awful situation this was. She'd never expected this when she escaped. She covered her face with her hand, trying to think what on earth she could do about this.

Noa said, "I thought you'd be happy to have a sister on your side."

Noa. She only saw the good things. She couldn't possibly understand all the difficulties. Esty ignored Noa and spoke to her sister. "Gila, if this is another of your crazy ideas, I think you'd better think about it again. Getting out is much harder than you think. It's much harder than I thought it would be. Once you've left, there's no going back. You'll be riddled with doubts and shame, and there'll be nothing you can do."

"You mean *you* were riddled with doubts. I won't be because I'm sure it's what I want."

"I was sure, too. But then things happened to make me have doubts."

"What things?"

Esty opened her mouth to answer, then closed it. This was hard. It was hard because Noa and Mark were listening. It was hard because she knew what her sister was like. When Gila got an idea into her head, she wouldn't let it go. But Esty had to try, for Gila's sake and for her own.

"Before I left, I knew there would be trouble with Mum and Dad. But I hoped we could get past that, or else that I'd be all right without them. Then I met them and I've never seen Dad so angry. It was awful. It made me feel so bad, I can't begin to explain what it did to me."

"I think I'm more ready for that. And besides, I won't be all alone. I'll have you."

"It's been so hard to get used to all the new things. Different clothes, television, there's so much that's different, and it's not all good, I can tell you."

"I'm not expecting paradise on earth, but I know it's the life I want. And I'm sure I can make it."

Esty sighed. "What did you want me to do?"

"Talk to Mum and Dad. Tell them I'm leaving anyway and they might as well give me their blessing. Tell them you'll look after me."

Again Esty sighed. "They'll think I put you up to this. They'll think it's all my fault. In case they don't blame me enough already, they'll be even more furious at me. Even if I can persuade them that I didn't cause it directly, they'll think you got the idea because I left first."

Gila paused, resting her clenched fist on her lips. Then she looked up and spoke quietly, her voice controlled. "So you're going to condemn me to marriage at sixteen and a life of drudgery because you've already got away and you don't want to make things worse between you and Dad. Do you think that's fair?"

"Gila, you know I love you and I want the best for you, but you're asking me to do something I can't do."

"You can. I know you can, and I'm asking you to do it. Please."

"Gila, when I left, I did it alone. No one I knew helped me. All I had was a phone number of someone on this side who could help. I can give you that phone number."

"Esty, you're nineteen. You're an adult. You can manage where I can't."

"Then you need to wait till you're an adult."

"But I can't because they want to marry me off. And that's your fault."

Esty was sobbing. "I don't know what to do. I'm torn between… everything."

Noa intervened. "I think Esty needs to think about this. It's been a shock for her. Why don't you go back home now, Gila, and come again tomorrow, or whenever you can?"

Gila looked despondent. "I can't get away again before next

125

week."

"Don't worry. They can't make you get married in a week, can they?" Noa looked at Esty for confirmation.

Esty shook her head.

"I'll go with you," Mark said, getting up.

Mark and Gila were making their way to the front door. Even in her confused state, Esty knew this was wrong. They shouldn't be going together. But she felt powerless to stop them. Through her tears, she called after them. "Don't sit next to each other on the bus."

Noa closed the door after them and returned to sit by Esty. "That was nice of Mark to accompany Gila back."

Esty didn't reply. After all the discussions they'd had together, Noa still didn't understand all the problems. A haredi girl didn't talk to a non-haredi man. Someone could see. People could assume all sorts of things that wouldn't be true. At least, Esty thought they wouldn't be true. She knew she couldn't trust her sister not to do something impulsive. Could she trust Mark? She wasn't sure about that, either.

Noa spoke again. "Esty, I'm sorry. I didn't realise how this would affect you. I thought you'd be happy to have someone from your family close to you. Seeing how it turned out, I think I should have let you talk to Gila alone."

Esty nodded and tried to smile through her tears. "I don't know what to do. Nothing seems right – not helping her and not abandoning her."

Noa gave Esty a squeeze with her arm. "Think about it. Sleep on it. Perhaps in the morning it won't seem so bad."

But in the morning, after waking up several times during the night, Esty felt just as miserable. Whatever she did now would be the wrong thing. People would hate her for it. People she loved. None of this would have happened if she hadn't escaped, herself.

She tried to put it aside during the day, and get on with other things. But she couldn't. The awful truth kept haunting her.

Mark was coming in the evening. Which side would he be on? Would he understand all the problems? Probably not.

"Where shall we go?" Mark asked when he arrived.

"Somewhere we can talk," said Esty.

"Park or coffee?"

"Park," said Esty. She didn't think coffee would help her to untangle the threads in her mind, and she wasn't in the mood to appreciate food.

They sat on a bench. Esty was oblivious to the people around. Even the noisy boys kicking a ball hardly registered.

"Esty, don't you think Gila deserves your help? She's in a difficult situation and you're the only one who can help her."

"But she's too young to decide something like that."

"She doesn't have much choice, does she? Your parents are forcing her to decide now."

Esty nodded. "I don't know what to do. It's so complicated."

"Doesn't seem so complicated to me. She wants to get out. She needs your help. You love her and want to do the best for her, so help her."

"You know it's not so easy. You heard what I said to her yesterday. And Gila is such an obstinate girl. She's always sure she knows what she wants, but sometimes she doesn't, or she changes her mind. This is something you can't change your mind about. Once it's done, it's done. There's no going back."

Mark nodded. "Gila is one feisty girl. She was telling me about her escapades last night. Like the time she and a friend bunked off school and took a bus to Tel-Aviv to see the sea."

"When did she tell you about that?"

"On the bus last night."

"So you sat together, after I said...."

"No. We sat on either side of the aisle. It was a bit awkward because people kept coming past, but she managed to tell me things."

"But Mark, someone could have seen, someone could be

reporting that Gila was talking to a strange, secular man. Don't you understand what you might have caused?"

"I understand that you're still under the spell of that world. You haven't left it yet. Not completely."

"Because the rest of my family is still there, and I don't want to harm them any more than I have already."

The ball rolled to Esty's feet. Even in her current mood, she couldn't help noticing it. She gasped, not because it hurt but because it surprised her and interrupted her thoughts.

Mark picked up the ball and threw it back to the children. "Esty, I can see this is hard for you. I think I can understand partly what a difficult position this puts you in. But Gila was right. You can't condemn her to the life you left. That wouldn't be fair. You have to help her get out."

***

During another sleepless night, Esty thought of a partial solution. She would discuss the whole issue with her mother the next time she came. Hopefully, that would be soon. Rivka might not know what to do either, but at least Esty could explain that she'd had no part in Gila's decision.

Deciding to talk to her mother didn't make Esty any more able to sleep though, because she began to worry about Mark. She thought back to the things he'd said about Gila. That she was feisty and got up to escapades. He seemed to be very keen on that. And if he liked Esty mostly for her looks – and Esty couldn't think of any other reason why he would like her – then he would like Gila just as much because they were so similar. Why was Mark so keen for Gila to leave the community? Could it be that Mark was falling in love with her little sister? Esty loved Gila very much. She didn't want to feel jealous of her, but she didn't want to share Mark with her or, worse still, to lose him altogether to her sister. She hoped she was imagining Mark's fascination with Gila.

***

Esty was pleased and nervous when her mother arrived on Tuesday. She decided to go with the pleased part.

"Mum, I'm so glad to see you. There's something I need to discuss with you."

"What's that, dear?"

"Let's go to my room."

As soon as they were seated in Esty's room, Esty began in the way she'd planned. "When I decided to leave the community, I decided by myself. I didn't tell anyone about it, not even someone in the family. It was my decision and my decision alone. You know that, don't you?"

"Yes…." Rivka was frowning, waiting to hear where this was leading.

"I had a visit from Gila on Saturday evening."

Esty felt her mother's eyes staring at her. The silence in the room suddenly made her load unbearable. She had to relieve herself of it, or at least to share it.

"Gila wants to follow me and be secular. And she wants me to help her do it."

Rivka didn't respond, so Esty added, "You know what Gila's like when she gets an idea into her head."

Rivka spoke softly. "What are you going to do?"

"I wish I knew. I know it's my fault. If I hadn't left, she wouldn't have thought of it. And you wouldn't have tried to push her into marriage now."

"That was Dad's idea. I wasn't so sure it would work, but he was adamant. He said we had to marry the girls off as soon as possible to stop them leaving."

"But I started it all. Without me, none of this would have happened. And I didn't even think about it when I left."

Esty felt her mother's arm squeezing her gently.

"Don't be so hard on yourself. You couldn't have foreseen everything."

"She's too young to make a decision like that."

Rivka shifted her position on the bed to face her daughter. "What if you talked to Dad and told him what happened? You could suggest he stops trying to make her marry now, and then she'll have time to rethink her decision."

Esty turned to gaze at the two pictures stuck to her wall, presents from Shirli and Roey. Roey's was indecipherable – a collection of curved lines. But Shirli's picture showed promise. "It's a brave lion," she had told Esty. Esty hoped the lion could give her courage for this forthcoming task. A meeting with her father would be very scary, but it was probably the best solution. She turned back to her mother. "All right, I'll try."

Then Rivka said something to make it even harder.

"Don't tell him I know about this."

***

Esty watched her father's face. Avi had arranged for them to meet in the same place as last time. Esty wished it could have been a different place. There were too many awful memories here. But there were differences this evening. The atmosphere was less heavy. Her father's face showed less anger, more resignation.

Esty began as she'd begun with her mother, but she struggled to keep her voice steady, afraid as she was of her father's reaction. Then she continued. "Dad, Mum, I'm telling you the situation as I know it. What you do about is of course up to you. But if I could make a suggestion…."

She looked at her father for approval. He gave a slight nod.

"…I would say the best thing would be not to force Gila into marriage now. Then she'll be able to wait and decide for herself when she's older and more mature."

"Thank you, Esty. Thank you for telling us this. I realise this has been hard for you, and I think you handled it well in the circumstances."

After her parents left, Esty had time to reflect. How different this meeting had been from the previous one. Not quite a normal conversation between parents and daughter, but much better than before, despite the news she'd had to impart to them. Her father had even paid her a compliment: "you handled it well."

At the appointed time, Esty left the flat to meet Noa, who arrived in her car.

"Glad you're here this time," Noa joked as she guided the car round the parked car in front and drove off. "How did it go?"

"Much better than last time. I really think things will sort themselves out between us in the end. And hopefully he'll do what I suggested and Gila will have plenty more time before she has to make any decision."

Little did Esty suspect what would happen just two days later.

Chapter Twenty

Esty attended Mark's synagogue again on Saturday. Now that she knew what to expect, the strangeness of the service was a bit less apparent. She supposed this was something she could get used to. And the congregants all seemed very pleasant.

They hadn't made any plans for the rest of the day, so they drifted round to Mark's place.

"I'm not sure what there is to eat there," said Mark. "Or if there's anything at all."

"That's all right," said Esty. "I'm not very hungry."

They found Claude in the flat, and for once he was alone.

"Oh là là! It is good that I buy baguette. Claude turned on the oven. I make the baguette hot and crusty and we eat it with Camembert, yes?"

"Sounds good," said Mark.

"And wine. We must drink wine to celebrate."

"Celebrate what? Esty asked.

There was a pause, and Esty thought she saw a silent message pass from Mark to Claude. Had she really seen Mark frown and give his head a slight shake, or had she imagined it?

"We celebrate the sun shine and the life is good."

The wine and the banter round the table helped Esty to relax.

"How come you're alone today, Claude?" she asked.

"Ah, my girl. She has too many family she has to visit. It is good she teach me Hebrew, but the family…." Claude shook his head.

"Why didn't you go with her?"

"They do not know about me. They are orthodox." Claude raised his eyebrows and turned up the palms of his hands. "She is too *compliquée*, this girl." Claude must have remembered who was sitting opposite him, because he added, "For me. I like simple girls."

Mark didn't respond, but Esty wondered whether he agreed with that sentiment. Perhaps he'd had enough of all the complications she had brought to their relationship.

Esty stayed in the flat with Mark all afternoon. They listened to some music on his laptop and looked at photos of Mark at different ages.

"This was on my bar-mitzvah." Mark clicked to enlarge a photo of a young-looking thirteen-year-old wearing a white shirt with a suit and tie, a black embroidered yarmulke and a shy smile.

"And this was on holiday in Cornwall." A younger boy in shorts and a tee shirt stood under a sign that showed NEW YORK 3147, JOHN O'GROATS 874 and HENDON 271."

Esty gasped. "I didn't know Hendon was such an important place."

"It isn't." Mark smiled. They change the sign for each tourist who pays for the photograph.

In Esty's current mood, she wondered if the smile showed that Mark was laughing at her for not knowing that. If she'd grown up in a normal environment, she probably would have guessed. Was Mark getting fed up with her, bored at having to explain everything?

Neither of them mentioned Gila. Esty was pleased that they didn't have to discuss her, as the topic of her sister had been causing tension between them. But she was surprised that Mark hadn't brought it up. It seemed as if Mark wanted to avoid it almost as much as Esty.

When the buses had started up after the Sabbath, Mark surprised Esty again. "I'm afraid I'll have to get rid of you for now, because I arranged to do something else this evening."

Of course Mark was free to do whatever he liked. It wasn't as if he was tied to Esty. But it wasn't like Mark to be so secretive.

What could he have planned to do that he didn't want to tell her?

Esty didn't feel it was her business to ask. She hoped her smile looked genuine. "That's all right. I need to do some studying tonight, anyway."

***

Esty had only been home for about half an hour when the doorbell rang. "I'll get it," she called out as she went to open the door. She froze when she saw the two people standing at the entrance to the flat. One was Mark. The other was Gila.

"Hello," Gila sang the word and she waved at Esty as if from far away. "Aren't you going to invite us in?"

Esty moved back for the two to enter, but still didn't believe what her eyes told her. This couldn't really be happening.

Gila led the way into the living room as if she owned it and the other two followed. Fortunately, Noa was out and Gadi was in his bedroom. Mark sat on the sofa next to Gila – too close, Esty thought. Esty faced them from an armchair and forced herself to collect her wits about her.

"Mark, I'll ask you first." Esty felt as if she had to tell off two naughty little children. She started with the one who was more likely to tell it straight. "What's going on?"

"Gila told you. She wants to leave the community. She's come here and she doesn't want to go back."

"What do you have to do with this?" It really was like dealing with children, dragging the truth out of them.

"Last week, when I accompanied Gila home on the bus, she asked me to help her leave. She said it wasn't fair that you wouldn't help and I thought she deserved to be helped. Only I don't really have anywhere to put her up and I know there's an extra bed in your room, so I thought you wouldn't mind having her with you at the beginning."

"Why didn't you tell me what you were going to do?"

"Because Gila asked me to keep it secret. Besides, you wouldn't have agreed."

"So you purposely went against my wishes."

"I've been hoping you'll accept the situation, now that it's a fait accompli."

"Gila, what do you have to say?"

Gila shrugged. "It's like Mark said. I know I want to leave. I don't want to wait till I'm eighteen. I want to leave now."

Esty wrung her fingers through her hair. Mark must have really fallen for Gila to agree to help her like that, otherwise he wouldn't have…. "Mark, you heard what I was worried about. You heard it last week and you heard it again when we met. How could you ignore all that and interfere in a private family matter?"

"Sometimes there are things that take precedence over the family. When a child is being abused, for instance, it's right to take the child away from the abuse."

Esty stared at Mark and frowned. "Are you suggesting that Gila has been abused?"

"No. But she's been forced into a lifestyle that she doesn't want."

"Every child is forced into a lifestyle of some sort. Who says the lifestyle you had is the right one? What about a child who is born into a very poor family? Would you take the child away from the birth parents and put him in a family with more money because it's a better lifestyle?"

Mark shook his head. "No. But Gila isn't a little girl. She's old enough to say what she wants, and she doesn't want the haredi life any more."

"She's old enough to say it. But is she old enough to make a lifelong decision? Does she really understand all the consequences?"

Gila spoke up. "Esty, really, how can you say that? You didn't know all the consequences when you left. You said so. You said you didn't even think about what it would do to the rest of the family. And another thing. I would have left anyway, even if I had to do it all by myself. It was nice to have Mark meet me, but I could have got here on my own like I did last week."

"Okay," Esty conceded. "But now I have to phone Mum and Dad."

"Why?"

"I have to tell them you're here. They're your guardians, not me. I can't be responsible for you against their will."

"But they won't agree to let me stay here."

"Then I won't agree to have you here."

"I don't think it's up to you to decide that. This isn't your home."

"It's not yours, either, and you can't stop me phoning."

***

Mark sat on the sofa beside Gila. He listened to the sisters bickering and felt sidelined. It was probably right of them to ignore him. What Esty had said was true. This was an internal family matter and he had no right to be involved in it. He shouldn't have agreed to help Gila.

But Gila had been so sweet on the bus the week before. He couldn't refuse after they got off when she asked to go somewhere quiet to talk. So he took her to Independence Park, where they sat on a bench and she used all her powers of persuasion.

"I'm going to leave anyway," she'd said. "I'm just asking you to make it a bit easier by coming with me." Her smile reminded him of Esty's although it contained more determination, more guile.

So he'd agreed to meet her this evening. He'd also agreed not to tell Esty about the plan. He'd hated deceiving Esty like that, but he'd promised Gila. He had told Noa, though, phoning her when he knew she'd be at work and away from Esty.

"Gila is welcome to stay in our flat with Esty," Noa had said.

"But Esty's going to need a lot of persuading over this, and I don't think I want to be there when Gila arrives. I'll go out that evening and hope that things have settled down by the time I return."

That had made Mark wonder about his part in this. But he'd already promised.

Now that he'd kept his promise, Mark decided, he was going to try not to take sides.

"Mark, please stop Esty from phoning our parents," Gila pleaded.

Mark replied softly but firmly. "I'm sorry, I can't do that. Esty has every right to talk to whoever she wants to."

***

Esty was pleased when her father answered the phone. She wanted him to hear this firsthand from her lips, so that he could be sure that this situation was not her doing, and that she was doing the best she could to be fair in difficult circumstances.

He took some time to reply, but Esty knew he was still there. She heard familiar voices in the background.

"It's late now," he said eventually. "Would it be all right with your hosts for Gila to spend the night there?"

"Yes, I'm sure it would. There's even a spare pull-out bed in my room... I mean, the room I'm staying in."

"In the morning – but please don't mention this to Gila – we'll come to talk to her. Will that be all right? Just answer yes or no."

"Yes."

"Will eight o'clock be all right?"

"Yes." The others would have left by then.

"You understand why I don't want you to tell Gila? I don't want her running away before we arrive."

"Yes."

***

Esty was in for another surprise when Noa returned.

"Hello, Gila," she said. "Lovely to see you."

"Noa!" In her amazement, Esty raised her voice a little too much. "You knew Gila was coming!"

"Yes, Mark told me."

"And you didn't tell me."

"I'm sorry, Esty, I was sworn to secrecy."

"It's like everyone knows our family business more than I do. Even Claude knows, doesn't he?" Esty said, turning to Mark as she remembered Claude's mention of a celebration and Mark's silent reproach of his friend.

Mark bit his lip. "I was worried. I'd promised to help Gila, but wasn't sure I'd done the right thing. Claude assured me that I had."

"He would."

"I'm sorry, Esty. I tried my best to be fair to everyone. I suppose I failed."

Esty felt sorry for Mark at that moment. "It's all right. I understand it was hard." Although she wasn't sure she really did understand.

***

Esty lay in bed listening to her sister's even breathing. It felt an age since she had slept with her sisters in the crowded little room. Gila had been excited about the new life she was expecting. Esty had told her about all the difficulties of beginning again, but she hadn't managed to put Gila off, or even to dispel some of her excitement.

Now Gila could enjoy a deep sleep while Esty stayed awake with her worries. All she had to do, she kept telling herself, was to keep Gila in the flat until eight. Surely that couldn't be hard. But you could never be sure with Gila. She always had something up her sleeve.

Then there was that other worry – Mark. He'd seemed very affectionate towards Gila, sitting beside her and smiling at her. Esty had tried to ignore all that and concentrate on her sister, but now that she was alone with her thoughts, the little things he said and did kept coming back to her. Just the way he'd let out an agreeing "Mmm," when Gila had said, "It's my life and you can't stop me." It was almost as if he felt proud of her for standing up to her older sister.

Perhaps Esty had been too hard on Mark. Perhaps she'd blamed him for things that were really Gila's fault. She knew how persuasive Gila could be.

All of that made Esty so very sad. She could feel Mark slipping away from her, and she didn't want to lose him.

***

The children were happy to see a new face in the morning. "Did you come from Mars, too?" Shirli asked.

Even Esty laughed at the question and Gila's confusion. "That's the way I described where we come from. It might be near, but in terms of the way of life it's light years away."

"You wear funny clothes," Shirli said pointing at Gila's long skirt and long-sleeved blouse.

"I'll get some new ones soon," Gila replied. She'd been a bit peeved when Esty hadn't let her wear any of her clothes, but for once she'd given in with the promise that she'd get some clothes of her own that day. Esty had her own reasons for wanting Gila to meet their parents in her normal clothes.

When the family left, Gila became impatient, wanting to phone Avi and to buy new clothes.

Esty had to rein her in. "We shouldn't phone Avi so early in the morning. Let him get settled at work first. And clothes shops don't open before about half past nine."

Fortunately, the doorbell rang at eight o'clock precisely. Esty showed her parents and a shocked Gila into the living room and left them to talk together, thankful that she'd completed her side of the bargain and could leave her parents to handle her reckless sister.

It took over an hour – much longer than either of the two meetings Esty had had with both her parents. Esty tried to ignore the sounds coming from the room, but there was no doubt that the meeting was a difficult one. When the door finally opened, her father looked as angry as she'd ever seen him, while Gila and Rivka had clearly been crying.

"Goodbye, Gila," her father said, making it sound like, "Goodbye for ever."

When their parents had left, Gila again amazed Esty by jumping up and down.

"Yes! I did it. I got away from them."

Despite knowing her sister inside out, Esty couldn't fathom this. Was it her age? Or her obstinacy? How could she be happy at having banished her parents from her life? At not being able to see her brothers and sisters again, as their father must surely have told her?

Esty still loved her sister and would do her best for her. Clearly love didn't mean the same thing for Gila. Perhaps it would as she matured. Perhaps she'd never learn to love anyone absolutely.

Suddenly, Esty felt sorry for Mark. If he was falling for Gila, he could be greatly hurt when he discovered how fickle she was.

Chapter Twenty-One

"Esty, I don't know how to put this. If we're going to London together we need to order our tickets, but I don't know... things might have changed. Do you still want to go with me?"

They were sitting side by side on a bench in the local park, glad that Jerusalem sometimes offered its inhabitants a respite from the heat, rewarding them with cool evenings – a rare prize missing in many other parts of the country. A young couple sauntered past, their arms entwined, their steps in perfect harmony.

More than a week had passed since he'd brought Gila to Esty, each day reinforcing Mark's doubts. He shouldn't have agreed to Gila's requests, he decided. He should have stood up to the girl, even though she was right to try to leave and he wanted to make it easy for her. It wasn't worth losing Esty because of her sister. Besides, Gila would have managed on her own. His part in the escape was minimal.

All this time, he hadn't even asked Esty what was happening with Gila. He'd been afraid to phone her, afraid he'd lost her already. Until Claude gave him a good talking to.

"If you do not talk, she think you do not care. If you talk, maybe she understand."

So he'd phoned Esty and arranged to meet her.

When Esty failed to respond to Mark's question, he was sure this confirmed his fears. Clearly Esty was searching for a way to end their relationship without hurting him too much. He could have saved her the trouble by telling her that such a way didn't exist, but before that, before they parted for ever, he had to ask after Gila. He had to know whether this step he'd helped with, albeit in a small way, was likely to work out well, even if his action had played a part in his downfall. So he left his question unanswered and asked another.

"How is Gila getting on?"

"Avi managed to get her into a boarding school," Esty said. "It wasn't exactly what she had in mind for herself, but we made it clear to her that if she didn't agree she'd be sent back home. I had to go and meet my parents again so that they could sign the agreement form."

"I'm sorry," Mark replied. "This is all my fault. I've been kicking myself."

"But it isn't. I know Gila would have got out anyway."

"So you're not angry with me?"

"I am. I don't think you should have interfered."

Mark dropped his hands onto his lap, feeling deflated. It was definitely all over, then.

"But I'll get over it," Esty continued.

"You mean, we can still be together?"

"If you still want me."

"Of course I want you. You know that, don't you?"

"I thought I did. But when Gila turned up, I thought you wanted her more."

"Gila? She's a lovely, intelligent, feisty girl. But she's just that – a girl. You're the one I want to go out with."

"Really? After all the silly things I've said and done? And the mess I've made of everything?"

"What mess?"

"Well, you know. I've changed my mind so many times about which direction I want my life to go in. I wouldn't blame you for not wanting to have anything to do with me again."

Mark took Esty's hand in his. "You're going through a difficult time. I didn't realise that at the beginning, but with all these new things going on and people from your past who suddenly appear, I can see how hard it is."

"But it's not fair on you. I keep changing my mind and you never know what to expect. You need a girlfriend who's stable.

Mark...." Esty's deep blue eyes exuded sadness and seriousness. "What I'm trying to say is, if you want to leave me now, I'll understand. I know how bad I've been."

Mark shook his head. "It's been hard, I admit. But I know you're a good person. You'll come through this in the end, and I'm going to wait until you do. Besides, I haven't been completely perfect either."

They gazed at each other for a while. Mark longed to wrap her up in his arms and feel her lips on his. He felt as if he wouldn't be able to hold back much longer. Did she feel the same way? He still wasn't sure, but maybe the time had come to risk it.

Mark would have kissed Esty right then if she hadn't saved herself by talking and breaking the spell.

"In that case, we'd better order those tickets."

***

"That's it," said Mark as they entered the departure lounge. "This is where we wait until it's time to board."

"I'm so glad you're here to tell me what to do," said Esty. "It's all very complicated. I was sure that woman at passport control was suspicious of me – the way she looked at me."

"Oh, don't worry. They always do that. They have to compare your photo with your face."

"I'm not surprised she double-checked, then. My passport photograph doesn't look anything like me."

Mark smiled. "That's normal. No one looks like their passport photo."

Esty had been looking around. "This place is big. Can we walk round it – look in all the shops?"

"Yes. Do you want to buy anything?"

"No, I just want to look. I bought my grandparents an embroidered tablecloth. I hope they like it."

She's like a child, thought Mark as they examined the shops

143

together. Still marvelling at everyday things that I take for granted – things that have been denied her up to now. What's going to happen when she grows up?

He hadn't seen much of Esty recently. Starting to teach at a new kindergarten had been tiring for her. And she was studying for her matriculation exams, too. He had asked her if she wanted to join him for services at his synagogue at the Jewish New Year, but she had declined, blaming tiredness, although he wasn't sure that was the whole reason. At Yom Kippur he hadn't asked her, knowing that the lack of transport would make it difficult for her to join him.

That had been his first Yom Kippur in the country and, although he'd been told that transport shut down completely on this special day – apart from occasional ambulances, it was still an amazing sight to watch people ambling along in the middle of the roads, the only wheeled vehicles being bicycles, children's push scooters and prams.

He'd continued to talk to Esty on the phone. She'd been friendly and talkative, but he still didn't feel sure of her. He supposed that was inevitable because Esty still wasn't sure of herself.

***

Esty touched her Oyster card on the sign and heaved a sigh of relief as the barrier opened and she hurried to pull her new suitcase through the gap before it closed again. She was feeling overwhelmed by all the new experiences of the day – the early start in the middle of the night, the pre-boarding procedures, the boarding itself, the anticipation until finally they were up in the sky and looking down over Tel-Aviv and the Mediterranean Sea, the bump as they landed and suddenly finding herself in another country where signs were all in English and they drove on the left. Not that she'd seen that yet; they'd travelled from the airport on the Underground, and although part of the journey had been above ground, she hadn't seen any streets close up. What she had noticed were the weird clothes some of the people wore. In particular, a lot of the young girls wore extremely tight and revealing shorts over tights, or mini-skirts that barely covered their buttocks. She found it hard to stop herself from staring.

Esty hadn't realised quite how enormous London was. It had taken them well over an hour to arrive at Hampstead Station, although the trains seemed to go very fast.

Fortunately, Mark had been with her all the time. He'd bought her an Oyster card for public transport in London and showed her how to top it up when necessary. He'd given her an Underground map and explained about all the different lines, and had warned her to check the destinations on the indicator boards, in case the first train to arrive wasn't the one she needed. He'd even offered to come out with her when they got to Hampstead Station, where her grandparents had arranged to meet her, before continuing to his parents in Hendon. But Esty preferred to meet them for the first time on her own. Later, when she knew them a bit better, she would introduce them to Mark.

There they were, standing by the ticket office, looking exactly like their photos but older and somehow sadder, despite their welcoming smiles. Esty wheeled her suitcase over to them. "Hello, I'm Esty."

They hugged her tightly and said they were "delighted" to meet her. Then they guided her to their rather posh-looking car. She slipped her case into the expansive boot and slid into the plush seat next to the stranger who'd raised her mother for eighteen years.

"Did you have a nice flight?" asked Naomi, this stranger she was to call Grandma.

"Well, I've never had any other flight, but it seemed fine."

"Oh yes, I forgot. It must have been exciting."

"It was. It was also confusing. I'm glad I had Mark to tell me what to do."

Naomi smiled. "I'm looking forward to meeting him. He sounds like a very nice young man."

"He is," said Esty, the corners of her lips automatically curling up.

The car glided along. Esty hadn't been in many cars in her life and certainly had never experienced such a smooth ride. The journey in the shared taxi that took her and Mark to Ben-Gurion airport had been nothing like this. Was it the way Harry, her grandfather, drove, or was it the car? Were all cars in Britain like this one? Esty looked out of the window and decided her grandparents' car was probably rather special, even here.

***

When they'd told her they lived in a flat, she hadn't imagined one like this. The front door opened onto a large hall, its floor covered with a wall-to-wall carpet thicker than any Esty had seen. Not that she'd seen many carpets at all; her parents' place didn't have one. They hardly had enough money for necessities, and certainly none left over for luxuries like that. Esty felt ashamed of her warm and practical but not very smart coat as Harry hung it up along with their smart ones in the well-varnished, fitted wardrobe.

Naomi directed the porter to the room that would be Esty's, and he carried her suitcase there. This must be to save the carpet from wheel marks, Esty assumed. He had done the same in the entrance hall of the block and on the way from the lift.

"I hope you'll be comfortable here," Naomi said as the porter made a discreet retreat.

"Comfortable! I'm sure I will. I could sleep on this carpet – it's so soft."

Esty looked around, amazed at what she saw. The furniture could have been antique. It was ornate, yet functional. The wallpaper, the pictures on the walls, the matching counterpane and curtains. Everything pointed to pure luxury. "I can't believe my mother left all this for a life of hardship."

Naomi's face suddenly looked more withered, her eyes – blue like Esty's – became sadder, making Esty sorry she'd mentioned her mother. "We lived in a house then, with a garden. Rosy was our only child. We did everything we could for her. We only wanted her to be happy."

Rosy, thought Esty, hearing this name for the first time. Her mother had even left her name behind. Esty lowered her voice, afraid to cause her grandmother more sorrow, but still longing to understand. "What happened?"

"She said she didn't care about creature comforts – about material things. She said there was no spirituality in our home and that was all that mattered. She was only eighteen when she went to Israel for two months between school and university. After a month, she wrote to say she was staying. We haven't seen her since."

Esty let a few seconds pass. "I don't know if this helps at all, but Mum told me recently – in secret – that she knows now she made a mistake. She thought she found spirituality but she learned it wasn't that at all."

"We made a mistake, too."

"What mistake?"

Naomi's head jerked, as if she'd suddenly woken up. "I'm so sorry, I shouldn't keep you standing here, especially when you've just arrived. Why don't you get washed and settled in, and then we can have lunch. I'm sure we have plenty to talk about."

Chapter Twenty-Two

Esty bit into her egg mayonnaise sandwich. Simple, tasty and somehow… English. Yes, this was something she'd probably want each time she came to England. She wondered what else would be added to that list. Definitely not salt and vinegar crisps. What a strange taste that was.

Esty had felt a bit guilty about going off today, so soon after meeting her grandparents, but they had assured her they didn't mind. "You don't want to spend all your time with a couple of old fogeys," Harry had joked.

The sandwich might have been simple, but this was no simple café. Each item bore the unique emblem of this place. Esty especially liked the cappuccino, topped with a crown made of chocolate powder.

People sat all around, talking in quiet undertones. Opposite her, Mark munched his own sandwich and sipped his cappuccino. Life was good.

"They're all so calm – it's amazing. Even the children are quiet and peaceful."

Mark nodded. "Israelis are much more in your face – for good and for bad."

"What's good about it?"

"Sometimes they get in the way. Other times they're there for you when you need them."

Esty immediately thought of the first time she'd met Mark. She'd needed him then. What if he hadn't been there? Would someone else have helped her? Quite possibly. Israelis were like that, Mark was right.

But London was so big, so special, so full of things to see. She looked out at the grounds below – forty acres of them, they'd said. Such a lot of green grass. And Mark had lived here all his life. "I can't believe you've never been to this place before."

Mark blushed a little and shrugged his shoulders. "When you live in London, you don't always think of doing the touristy things. Anyway, when you've seen one palace you've seen them all, basically. They all have large rooms, old pictures, four-poster beds. The stories behind the palaces are what make them interesting."

"Are there many palaces around the world?"

"Oh yes. Not in Israel, because there were no kings and queens there in the Middle Ages or later."

"If I ever see any others, I'll always compare them to Buckingham Palace – my first one. Unless my grandparents' place counts as a palace."

"Is it that grand?"

"Well, you'll see it this evening. It's not as big as this, of course, but it's fantastic. It's got enormous rooms and thick carpets and wallpaper and lovely pictures and antique furniture."

"They must be very happy there."

"But they're not – not really. My grandma talked to me about it. She keeps a lot hidden inside. She was really happy to have someone from the family she could confide in."

"Well don't tell me any secrets."

"They're not secrets, really. Only things she doesn't want to burden anyone else with."

"Like what?"

"Well, I suppose it all comes from the fact that they were both born very soon after the Second World War and they're both children of Holocaust survivors. In fact, that's how they met – in a club for second generation survivors. She said no one talked about the war when they were growing up because it was too close – everyone who'd lived through that time wanted to move on and not dwell on those awful years. But for their

149

parents it was as if life didn't exist before they came to England. Not only did they hardly mention the camps; they didn't discuss their lives before the war, because the people they'd lived with were no longer alive."

"That must have been hard on their children – not knowing their parents' background. It's almost as if they didn't know who their parents were."

"Exactly. And as children growing up, they didn't have anyone to share with – not till they met each other. And they never managed to involve their daughter in their feelings – only in their wealth. They started a business together and made a lot of money, but they didn't have any friends or family. And they tried to protect their daughter, making her feel that they didn't have any emotions. That was their first mistake. The second, Grandma said, was that they were sure they didn't want religion. They saw it as the source of evil – something that keeps people apart. Now they're not so sure. They think in moderation it can be good."

"I agree with that."

"I know. I'm beginning to think you were right all along. Extremism of any sort is dangerous."

Mark reached his hand along the table and met Esty's. Placing it on top, he gave a gentle squeeze and they gazed into each other's eyes.

***

Mark held Esty's hand as they strolled out of Buckingham Palace grounds. The café had been expensive, but Esty was worth the expense. And he loved the way they were coming together – in thinking and in emotion. He needed to stop feeling hurt, as he had when she'd said she couldn't believe he hadn't been there before. She hadn't meant it as an accusation and he shouldn't have taken it in that way. When she looked into his eyes like that, he could tell how she felt about him, he thought. He hoped.

Mark bought the tickets for a tour of the Houses of Parliament and they ambled down to the riverside to fill in the time before their tour began. As they stood watching the activity on and beside the river, Esty continued to enthuse about Mark's native city and Mark did his best to brush his doubts away.

The parliament tour was fascinating. Mark was interested to hear about the origins of various items and practices. He particularly liked the statues of all the past leaders, and marvelled at the likenesses. Esty also took great interest in the tour, but her comment at the end, as they handed back their identity tags, pleased him greatly.

"Can you take a tour like this of our parliament?"

"The Knesset? Yes, I've been on that tour. It's also worth going on. You find out a lot on it."

"I'd like to do that," Esty said. "After all, this is foreign history – to me, anyway. But the Knesset is part of the history of my country."

Mark smiled. He'd started to worry that Esty was falling in love with the country he'd only recently left. He was pleased that she still identified more with his adopted country.

It was the following day when the bombshell fell.

Chapter Twenty-Three

"Good afternoon, sir."

Mark found it hard to get used to this subservience. He mumbled a reply, making sure to give his shoes a good wipe on the mat before stepping on the plush carpet.

The porter held the lift door open, and Mark nodded his thanks as he stepped inside. The porter pressed the button and retreated.

Mark had experienced all this the previous evening when he'd arrived for dinner and met Esty's grandparents. He'd been nervous because of it, unsure whether their wealth had made them snobbish and artificial. But they turned out to be warm and unpretentious, and the evening had been easy and pleasant.

Today, like yesterday, Naomi opened the door to Mark with a smile. "How lovely to see you again. Esty's all ready and waiting, and the sun is shining. Enjoy yourselves."

Esty looked radiant, all the way to Hampstead Heath and as they walked along within the borders of the large park. "It's so big," she said. "I wish there was something like this in Jerusalem."

"Jerusalem is a beautiful and fascinating city," said Mark. "It's amazing how much it holds in such a small space. But you're right – it doesn't have any large parks like this. Everything's on a much smaller scale there."

When they sat down on the grass on a hill, where the panorama included much of the city, Esty became pensive. "My grandparents suggested something to me today. I'm not sure what to do about it."

"What did they say?"

Esty glanced at Mark and bit her lip. "They want me to

move to London. They'd like me to come and live with them, so they can look after me as they would have done to my mum if she hadn't gone away. They were going to suggest the same to Gila, but that would be more complicated because she's under eighteen, and they agreed she should finish her education at the boarding school before thinking of moving countries."

Mark felt a jabbing pain, as if a shard had gone through his heart. Just when he was beginning to feel more sure of Esty and her feelings for him, she was going to leave him. How could he survive that?

But this wasn't about him. He had to put his feelings aside. This was about Esty. It was her decision. "What about *your* studies?"

"I can study in London. They'll pay for it. And there's so much opportunity in London."

Mark sat back on the grass, resting on his hands, and gazed across at the London skyline. The London Eye peered back at him. Yes, London had a lot to offer. But so did Jerusalem, and there he felt freer, more independent, better able to manage his life.

"Mark, would you ever consider coming back to London?"

Mark closed his eyes for a moment. When he opened them, the familiar panorama was still there. "I don't know. I'm only beginning to settle down in Jerusalem. I had several reasons for moving away. The difficulty of living with my parents was only one of them."

"What else was there?"

"In England I was always aware of being in a minority, especially at school. I was sick of it, even though I didn't experience any real hostility. I had enough of being different. I guess it's a hangover from childhood – the longing to be the same as the others."

Mark thought back. "There was one teacher. Miss Heathcliff."

"Miss Heathcliff? Is that what you called your teachers –

Miss and Mrs and Mr?"

"Yes. What else could we have called them?"

"By their first names. Children always call teachers by their first names in Israel."

"Really? How odd. I suppose it makes kids relate to the teacher in a different way – as another human being rather than a monster."

"Tell me about Miss Heathcliff. I bet she taught Geography."

"She did actually, funnily enough. She always set homework on days when I was away for the Jewish holidays. Then she'd write in her list of marks NGI for not given in. It made me feel as if it was my fault that I hadn't done the homework."

"Couldn't you have gone to a Jewish school?"

"My parents didn't believe in religious separation in schools, and I understood that. It didn't stop it being hard, though. But you, coming as an adult, probably won't feel the same way.

"Esty…." Mark turned to look at the girl he yearned for. She looked so perfect and unattainable perched on the grass, her legs folded to the side, her hair hanging loose on the other side. "You have to decide what's best for you. This could be a wonderful opportunity for you."

"I need to think about it."

Mark tried not to think about it for the rest of the afternoon. They walked around in the park. At the pond, they came across a family with several children playing with boats. Esty gasped as she recognised the haredi "uniform" – the black skullcaps and long sideburns on the boys and the black coat, hat and beard on the father. She was even more surprised when she heard them speak.

"They speak English," she whispered to Mark. "With English accents."

"Of course," said Mark. "They live here."

"I didn't know there were any here."

"In London? There are plenty of them. If you went to Golders Green you'd see lots. They used to live only in Stamford

154

Hill, my parents told me. But they've spread out."

"I didn't know," Esty said again. "So even in London you can't get away from them."

***

They parted to dress for the evening, and Mark met Esty at Hendon Central Station and took her to his parents' house.

It was about six in the evening when the couple arrived. Esty didn't really know what to expect from Mark's parents and worried they might be critical of her, but they seemed warm and welcoming.

"Do call me Sharon," Mark's mother said when Esty stumbled over "Mrs Langer."

Keith, Mark's father, also seemed pleasant enough, although he left most of the talking to his wife. He offered them drinks before the meal, and Esty agreed to a small sherry. The house was comfortable, but not as luxurious as that of her grandparents.

They sat down to a meal that started with chopped herring on a bed of egg slices and continued to fresh, baked salmon with buttered small potatoes and fresh asparagus.

"Do pour some lemon sauce on the salmon," said Keith, handing Esty a glass dish with a handle and a spout on a matching plate.

"This is all so wonderful," Esty said. "I didn't know potatoes could taste so delicious."

"They're new potatoes," Sharon explained.

Esty didn't really know the significance of the potatoes being new, but gathered it made them into some sort of delicacy.

The meal ended with trifle, raspberries on a base of sponge cake moistened with sherry. Esty revelled in the mixture of sweet tastes, the cake and fruit with custard, and the cream topping.

"You've worked hard on this meal," Esty said.

"I hope you like it," said Sharon.

"I certainly do."

"Do you know what they call sponge cake in Israel?" Mark asked his mother, knowing what the answer would be.

"No."

"English cake."

"That's funny." Sharon smiled. "It's like Americans calling chips French fries." She turned back to Esty. "So Mark tells me you used to be haredi."

It took Esty a moment to understand the word the way Sharon pronounced it with a hard h-sound and the stress on the second syllable instead of the third. "Oh, yes. In fact, it's only been four months since I left the community."

"Really? That must have been very hard, breaking away from everything you knew."

"It wasn't easy," Esty admitted.

"What about your family? Tell me about them."

Esty listed all nine of her siblings, giving their names and ages.

"That's quite a large family," said Sharon.

Esty shrugged her shoulders. "It's pretty average where I come from."

"I understand you haven't been able to see them since you left."

"That's right. Except for my sister, Gila, who decided to leave, too."

"Do you miss all the others?"

Esty nodded. "Terribly. I knew I'd probably be cut off when I left, but I hoped that it wouldn't happen."

"So you're very much alone – rather like an orphan."

Not wanting to sound sorry for herself, Esty looked for a positive outcome of leaving her parents and siblings. "But at least I've found some new family."

"Your grandparents?"

Esty nodded. "They've been wonderful to me and I can't

156

thank them enough. In some ways, I'd feel as if I was being selfish if I didn't stay with them."

"Stay with them? How do you mean? Permanently?"

"Yes, I… didn't you know? Sorry, I thought Mark would have told you. They want me to stay in London and study here instead of in Jerusalem."

Esty felt confused. How could it be that Mark hadn't told his parents about this new development? It must mean that Mark wasn't as interested in staying near Esty as she was in staying near him. For her, the fact that she might be separated from Mark was the biggest thorn in the bed of roses. For Mark, she assumed, she was just another girlfriend, the sort that come and go.

"Really? What do you think of that?"

"Well, it's very tempting. Their flat is comfortable and what I've seen of London is fantastic."

Sharon was smiling. Esty wondered why.

"It sounds like a very good idea, Esty. And maybe if you come to live here, Mark would come back, too."

Now Esty understood why Sharon was so happy. She wanted her son back. She wanted him to be close to her where she could mother him and possibly, as Mark had said, control him. And she thought that if Esty decided to live in London, he would go back to London to be with her. She seemed to have it all worked out in a flash. If Esty didn't stall her line of thought, she'd be cancelling their tickets for the flight back to Israel or a least persuading them to do so.

"I haven't decided yet. I have to think about it."

"Of course. It's a big step. But it could be a wonderful opportunity for you."

***

Mark accompanied Esty back to the station together.

"You're parents are very nice," said Esty. "And they went to a lot of trouble for me."

"I'm glad you like them. I think they like you, too."

"Mark, why didn't you tell them about my grandparents' suggestion?"

They walked on a bit before Mark replied.

"I'm trying very hard to leave me out of the equation. This is a decision you have to make for yourself; it's nothing to do with me. I know how I feel about it all, but I don't want to influence your decision. And I knew that if I told my parents, they'd immediately be in favour of the plan, because they'd see it as a way to bring me back to them. But I know what it would be like if I went back. I don't want to lose my independence."

They'd stopped walking and stood in the middle of the pavement on Watford Way, a stone's throw from the station. Traffic streamed past and pedestrians walked round them, but Esty hardly noticed. She reached up to put her arms round Mark's shoulders and gave him a quick kiss on the cheek. Then she would have removed her arms and taken a step back, but she couldn't. She felt herself being squeezed close to Mark. She felt his hands on her back, pulling her towards him. And she felt his warm lips on hers, his tongue touching hers.

Rather than tensing up, Esty relaxed in Mark's arms. For a moment, this seemed just perfect. Then they broke away and Esty felt less sure.

Mark, too, it seemed. "I'm sorry, Esty. I don't know what came over me. You probably hate me for doing that."

"No, I… I'm a bit confused. In fact, I'm very confused. But I'll work it out. I promise."

Esty ran to the station without so much as a goodbye.

***

Mark traipsed back to his parents' house with a weary step. What a fool he was. Without thinking properly, he'd somehow taken Esty's little hug as permission to go much further than she'd wanted or intended. He felt so ashamed. How could he ever look Esty in the eye again after everything had gone so wrong?

Sharon greeted Mark from the kitchen door as he opened the front door with his key. He hoped she couldn't see the sadness on his face across the dark corridor.

"Would you like a cup of tea?"

"No thanks, Mum. I think I'll go to bed. I'm feeling rather tired."

Mark didn't fall asleep for a long time. He rolled over several times, literally kicking himself for his stupidity.

In the morning, he tried to sound as perky as usual. "I think I'll go through some of the things in my room," he announced after breakfast. "See what I want to take back with me." He escaped back upstairs, glad of an excuse to be alone and wondering how he was going to explain the sudden disappearance of Esty from his life. He was surprised when Sharon called him to the phone. Especially when she told him the call was from Esty.

His heart was beating fast as he answered the phone. Was this the goodbye Esty had omitted to say last night?

"Mark, I think we need to talk. Where can we go?"

Mark looked through the window at the rain and grey skies that reflected his mood. At least Esty wanted to talk, even if it was only to say her goodbye face to face.

"It had better be indoors. How about lunch in a restaurant? Could we meet at Golders Green Station? There are plenty of restaurants around there."

***

Mark was careful not to touch Esty as they ambled along Golders Green Road. They were both quiet, except when they passed some men dressed in black, all holding their hats on against the strong wind.

"You're right," Esty said. "You can't get away from them here."

"No, you can't." For a moment, Mark let a slight smile break through his sadness. Maybe all was not quite lost. "The funniest thing is when it rains in Jerusalem and they all go around with plastic bags on their heads to protect their hats."

Mark turned to Esty and once again silently rebuked himself. Esty wasn't smiling. Of course she wasn't. For him, seeing men wearing plastic bags on their heads was hilarious. For Esty, it was normal. Her own father probably did that.

"I'm sorry, Esty. I didn't think."

"No, you're right," said Esty. "It is funny when you look at it from the outside, which is what I need to do. And it would be no good if you had to think hard about everything you were planning to say to me."

They decided on an Italian restaurant and chose a corner table. Then they had to make their choices from the long menu. Esty chose Pizza Margherita. Mark decided on spaghetti with tomato and basil, although he didn't feel at all hungry. When asked what they wanted to drink, they requested water.

As soon as the waitress went off with their order, Esty began to talk.

"Mark, last night I made a decision about where I want to live, and I told my grandparents this morning."

Mark raised his eyebrows as he looked up at her, filled more with apprehension than with hope.

"I'm going to stay in Jerusalem. It's my home; it's where I've always lived. And it's where my parents live, and my brothers and sisters, including Gila who is now my responsibility. One day I hope we'll be able to breach the rift in our family, because I still love them all dearly. If I move away, I might never see them again."

Mark still didn't know what to feel. Hope seemed to be gaining on apprehension. Surely if Esty was going to stay in Jerusalem, she must have forgiven him for last night. But

160

possibly not. Just because they were living in the same town, that didn't mean they'd still be together.

"Esty, I have to ask you. Do you want us to carry on being friends?"

"Yes, I do. Very much so."

"Even after what I did last night?"

Esty twiddled the serrated-edged knife that had appeared in front of her. "I had a long conversation with my grandmother when I got back last night. I'm afraid I kept her up long after her usual bedtime. She told me a lot about love and emotions. I was brought up not to think about these things. Any time I did think about love, I thought I would choose a husband out of about three who were suggested and after meeting him two or three times. And I hoped I would grow to love the man I chose after we married.

"Now I can see that it's all different on the other side. And I think I understand much better what I've been doing to you – making you hold back, against your instincts. It wasn't fair of me to make it so hard for you, just because of the hang-ups I brought with me from the other world. The men I met there held back, too, because they were brought up with the same hang-ups. But I should never have expected you to do the same."

Mark reached over the table to hold Esty's hands, and looked straight into her eyes. The apprehension had gone, and the hope had been replaced by assurance. And love.

"I love you, Esty."

"I love you, too."

When the waitress reappeared with their meals, Mark asked for a glass of white wine each. "This is a celebration," he explained to Esty as the waitress went for the wine and glasses. "A new phase in our friendship."

Esty's mouth opened at the size of the glass full of wine. "I'm not sure I could drink all that."

"Just drink as much as you want. Don't worry about getting

drunk; I'll be here to look after you."

They tucked into their meals. Then Mark asked, "What about your grandparents? They must be very disappointed you're not staying in England."

"They are. I felt awful telling them. But they understand. And we discussed Gila, too. They're hoping she'll stay with them next summer. I think that's a good idea. It'll be good for them to meet another member of the family. But also, they'll see what a handful she can be. Maybe they'll think twice about having her to live with them."

"Gila might change as she matures."

"Maybe she will. Maybe she'll decide to stay in England. Or maybe she'll think like me, about the other reason why I don't want to live with my grandparents."

"What do you mean?"

"I think if I lived with them, they'd be too close. They'd mean well, but they wouldn't let me be myself. They'd want to protect me too much."

Mark thought back to his own experience of living with his parents as an adult. "I can understand that."

"I think that's also one of the reasons why my mother left. But she wasn't mature enough to be independent. She left one over-protective environment and ended up being part of another. I think I'm ready to manage in an open society."

Mark beamed at Esty. She really had come a long way from the frightened girl he had helped that afternoon in the post office.

Chapter Twenty-Four

Mark rang the doorbell with some trepidation. It was the first Saturday evening after he and Esty had returned to Jerusalem and they'd both been busy, he with work that had been piling up in his absence, she with the kindergarten and her studies. He would really rather have had a quiet evening alone with Esty, but he knew this was important. Still he worried that he wouldn't know what was and wasn't expected of him. Shaking hands, for instance. Presumably, he shouldn't.

Esty opened the door and led Mark to the living room. Noa and Gadi had kindly let them use it. As they entered, Esty said, "This is my mother, Rivka."

Rivka approached Mark. "Pleased to meet you, Mark," she said and extended her hand.

Mark looked at her and hesitated. Her long skirt and sleeves with the black tights stood out more here, where the weather was still warm, than they did on the haredi women they'd seen in autumnal London. Surely this woman wouldn't shake a man's hand.

Rivka smiled and Mark was touched by the similarity to Esty's smile. "It's all right. You can shake my hand." While they shook, she explained, "I haven't shaken a man's hand for a long time, but I do remember when I did that without even thinking about it, and I decided it was the right way to begin our friendship."

Mark relaxed enough to be able to observe the person behind those telling clothes. She was shorter than Esty but really very much like her. They had the same blue eyes and slim bodies. Surprising after all those births.

They sat round the dining table, on which Esty had put out

cold drinks, biscuits on a paper plate and paper cups. All in honour of her mother, Mark observed, knowing that Rivka wouldn't eat or drink from the china in this non-kosher home.

"I've heard a bit about you, Mark, and I'm longing to hear more. How long have you been in the country?"

Mark delighted in hearing English spoken with an accent very much like his. The fact that it was a little more refined than his probably reflected the area she came from and the school she attended. As the conversation continued, Mark warmed to this woman and almost forgot the huge gap between them that would normally prevent them from ever having a meaningful conversation.

"How was your trip to England?" Rivka asked.

"Wonderful," Mark replied. "You know, when I lived with my parents, towards the end, I was longing to get away and make a life for myself. But now that I've become more independent, I really appreciated going back for a bit. Even the way they spoilt me felt good. I wouldn't want to live with them any more, but I loved going back for a visit."

Rivka lowered her eyes to the table. "I haven't seen my parents for twenty years."

"I know – I met them. They're very nice people."

"They didn't deserve what I did to them."

"Maybe you could make it up to them and visit them now."

"I think it's too late for that now."

"It isn't, Mum," Esty joined in. "I'm sure it isn't. They really want to see you again."

"But they've always been so much against religion. They wouldn't want to see me like this." Rivka turned her fingers towards her long dress."

"They've mellowed since then, Mum. I know they'd accept you as you are, now. Just tell them you're coming. Tell them what they have to do to make it comfortable for you. They'd do anything to see you again."

Rivka raised her shoulders. "I don't know where we'd get the money for the flight."

"Mum, you know that's not a problem for them."

Rivka shook her head. "I couldn't possibly accept money from them."

"Are you going to deny them their wish because you're too proud? One day, it'll really be too late."

Rivka looked down again and bit her lip.

All too soon, Rivka had to leave to return home. They stood up and Rivka shook Mark's hand again. "I'm delighted to have met you, Mark. I think you're a fine man and I'm very glad my daughter has found your support and friendship."

Esty saw her mother to the door and then returned to the room and sat beside Mark at the table. "That went well. I'm so pleased."

"Your mother is a lovely woman. I really like her."

"Despite the way she looks?"

"You know, after a while I forgot the strange clothes. And the wig. If you don't think about it and look for the gap between the hair and the head, it looks as if she has a really nice hairdo."

"You know, growing up I was used to the wigs. All the married women I knew wore wigs. Now, when I think about it, the whole idea is so ridiculous."

"You mean, because it comes from the idea that a woman shouldn't show herself off to anyone but her husband?"

"Right, so she covers her hair up with a wig that makes her look more attractive than she does without it. It doesn't make sense."

"That's what happens when people keep a law to the letter, rather than thinking about the real reason for it – the spirit of the law."

***

Rivka was back on Tuesday evening. Esty was delighted because she needed guidance from anyone who could help.

"Your friend, Mark, is a lovely young man," Rivka began, settling herself on Esty's bed. "I'm so pleased you found him."

"So am I," said Esty. "Mum, can I ask you something?"

"Of course."

"What can you tell me about love?"

Rivka took a moment to reflect. "I wasn't in love with Dad when we got married. It all happened too quickly for that. The matchmaker brought us together and I had to say yes or no. I said yes, he said yes and suddenly we were married and I was still only eighteen."

"And he was nineteen."

"Right. The laws were all new to me then, but I was determined to keep them all. I worked especially hard, cleaning and cooking for the Sabbath, having everything just right. And I had to work outside our home, too. There wasn't much time to think about love."

"So you can't tell me anything about love?"

Rivka shook her head. "I didn't say that. Occasionally, I did think about love, and I realised it had crept up on me gradually. It wasn't just that I'd grown used to living with Dad. I really did care for him and… love him. I still do. When you asked me, that time, why I didn't leave when I realised I didn't believe in the haredi way of life any more, I said I couldn't leave the children, but I also couldn't leave Dad. I couldn't imagine life without him. He and I belong together. That's love."

"How do you know when you're in love?"

"Lie back, close your eyes and bring up an image of your man. Imagine life with him – the conversations, the things you might do together and the romance. The good times and the bad. Then imagine life without him. Would you be just as happy, or would you always be grieving, angry with yourself for having missed the opportunity?"

They sat in silence for a while before Esty said, "Thank you, Mum. I'll think about that."

It was then that Rivka told Esty the latest news.

The following evening, Esty caught Noa in the kitchen and asked her the same question.

"What can you tell me about love?"

Noa left the saucepan soaking in the sink and went to sit opposite Esty. "Love is hard to describe. I love my children and I love Gadi, but the two things are very different. It's my love with Gadi that you want to hear about, I expect."

Esty nodded.

"I know people get it wrong sometimes. They think they're in love but they aren't really, or they are in love but they fall out of love. But Gadi and I knew each other for three years before we decided to get married. We spent a lot of time with each other. I knew everything about him – his good points and his weak ones. And he knew mine. When I thought about spending the rest of my life with him, I knew it was what I wanted. I knew it was right for me. I don't know how else to describe it. It's just something you know."

"Do you think I'm in love with Mark?"

"From where I am, from the outside, I think you two are right for each other. You have a lot in common, but are different enough to be suited to each other. And when I see the way you look at him and hear what you say to him and what you say about him, it seems to me that you're in love with him. But only you can tell if you're really in love."

***

Two days later, his flatmates all planning to be away for the coming weekend, Mark invited Esty for a Friday night meal – just the two of them. "I warn you, I'm not a gourmet cook," he'd told her on the phone." "Neither am I," she replied, laughing.

The previous evening's folk dancing session had been the best ever. Esty's presence had made all the difference. She was no longer afraid to hold his hand, nor even to let him hold her round the waist. And at last she was able to relax and let him guide her when she didn't know the steps.

Mark worked hard all day, tidying, cleaning, shopping and now cooking, hoping that his meagre skills would suffice. He kept it simple – roast chicken and potatoes, humus, fresh salad and fresh fruit to follow. Still, he worried. What about lighting candles for the Sabbath and the other traditions? Would she want to perform them, or did she still spurn them?

Fortunately, Esty solved that problem as soon as she arrived. "Shall I light the candles?"

When the time came, Esty went over to the waiting candles, struck a match and lit them. Then she waved her hands over them three times and covered her face. It warmed Mark's heart to hear her reciting the blessing, exactly as his mother had always done.

During the meal, Esty filled Mark in on her latest news. "My mother paid me another visit, in secret."

"She managed to get away during the week?"

"Yes. I think my father knows she's seeing me, and he's turning a blind eye to it. So she told me my sister – the one whose engagement was broken off – now has another suitor – someone who doesn't mind what I did. And now she's pleased the other one left her, because she's really in love with this one."

"I *am* glad."

"And, do you know what else my mother said? She said my father is beginning to get used to what happened. She thinks, soon – not yet – he'll agree to have normal contact with me."

"That's wonderful, Esty. I'm really pleased for you."

"They even discussed going to England next year. Apparently my dad might be able to get a job there for the summer as a cantor, filling in for one who wants to visit his family in different parts of the world. They might even be able to take all the kids."

"Gosh."

"I heard from my grandparents, as well. They've got involved in a charity for children. They're not only donating money to the charity, but actually working for it, too. I think they've really accepted my decision not to stay with them, and they're excited about being able to help those less fortunate. And they've made some good friends through the charity."

"That's great. They're such nice people. I'm glad they're happy."

"Yes. And I must tell you what happened to Mrs Greenspan." Esty looked sideways at Mark with a smile that was almost a grin. Mark had the feeling she was struggling to prevent herself from laughing out loud.

"What happened?"

"She's under house arrest, awaiting trial."

"No! Why?"

"You remember how she kidnapped me?"

Mark nodded. "How could I forget?"

"Well, she kidnapped another girl who escaped like I did. Or at least she thought she did."

Mark felt a grin of his own coming on. "Go on."

"She made a mistake. It was the wrong girl! And this girl's boyfriend and another friend were coming out of a shop and saw what happened. They grabbed Mrs Greenspan and her accomplice and called the police, who kept them behind bars for a whole night."

"Wow!"

"No one wanted the task of making sure she stays indoors. She's not well liked in the community. But they found a family member who had no choice."

"Wow!" Mark said again. "How did you hear this?"

"My mother told me. It's all over the community."

"Well, if anyone deserved that, it's her."

"Anyway, that's enough of my news. What's happening with you?"

"I've been looking into buying a small flat. I think I have enough money for the deposit now."

That smile again. The usual one. "That's wonderful. I *am* pleased for you. If you want any help searching, I could come with you."

"Thanks." Mark's plans actually went further than that, but the rest would depend on Esty.

They finished the meal, chatting easily together about their growing circle of common friends and acquaintances.

"Claude seems to be in love."

"Claude is always in love."

"This time it's different. He said…" Mark paused to change accents. "'Mark, *mon ami*, I thought I know everything about love, but I know nothing. Nothing at all. Now I know. Love, it is Brigitte.'"

"She's French, too?"

"Yes, you should see how they look into each other's eyes and go, '*Je t'aime.*' It's so sweet."

As always, Mark loved to see Esty's smile. But, was he imagining it or was the smile not quite as radiant as usual?

***

Esty was having trouble keeping the selfish thoughts out of her mind. When Mark mentioned buying a flat, it occurred to her that they could buy one together. With help from her grandparents that she knew would be forthcoming, they could buy a larger flat in a better area. But something rather important would need to happen before Esty could suggest that. And it would have to happen before Mark signed the contract on a place he could afford to buy on his own.

And Esty was delighted to hear about Claude, of course. But she also felt a slight pang of jealousy. And from the way Mark was eyeing her, she thought he might realise how she was feeling. Time to change the subject.

"That was a lovely meal, Mark. You went to such an effort for me. And now you must let me clear up."

"Wait. Not yet. There's something I want to say first. Let's go and sit on the sofa." Mark took Esty's hand and led her to the sofa.

Esty's heart began to beat faster. Was Mark going to say what she thought he might say? It suddenly seemed as if this could be the right time. She hoped it was.

They sat down, side by side, on the sofa.

Mark turned to face her. "Esty…"

Esty saw, in Mark's eyes, the love that warmed her heart. But she also saw him fighting with himself. She knew he was scared of being rejected. She realised she had to do something to make it easier for him, to show him that it would be all right. Not to do it instead of him, though. That would make him feel as if he'd failed. In any case, she'd made so many changes to her life recently, she wanted Mark to be in control of this one. And maybe Mark felt insecure because she hadn't let him get too close to her before. Except for that time in London, and he was probably still reeling from that, afraid he'd gone too far. But now… now was the time.

"Mark, you don't have to hold back because of me any more."

Esty continued to watch Mark's face. She saw his anxiety dissolve, to be replaced by calm rapture. So beautiful. She hoped he would go slowly, to draw this moment out as long as possible. She didn't want it ever to end.

As if he heard her thoughts, Mark's hands edged round her waist to join behind her. Slowly, gently, he lifted her to a standing position. Esty stood on tiptoe and put her arms round his shoulders. Then their lips met and it felt perfect, as if this was always meant to be, as if she'd finally found everything she'd been searching for.

Their lips parted but they remained together, embracing.

"Esty, will you marry me?"

Her body was tingling, her lips on fire, but her reply came out clearly and confidently. "Yes."

They fell into a tight, warm embrace, and Esty felt ecstatically happy and safe in the protection of Mark's strong arms. She was no longer alone in an alien world. No longer straddling the fence, neither here nor there. Now she was half of a union in a world where she belonged.

THE END

Fantastic Books
Great Authors

Meet our authors and discover our exciting range:

- Gripping Thrillers
- Cosy Mysteries
- Romantic Chick-Lit
- Fascinating Historicals
- Exciting Fantasy
- Young Adult and Children's Adventures

Visit us at:
www.crookedcatpublishing.com

Join us on facebook:
www.facebook.com/crookedcatpublishing

CPSIA information can be obtained at www.ICGtesting.com
Printed in the USA
BVOW04s1141170615

405007BV00001B/4/P